The Holiday Hotel

# Jack Taylor Cases:
# The Holiday Hotel

*by C. N. Wynn*

Written by Christian N. Wynn
Cover illustration by Nick Street
Edited by Stefanie Spangler-Buswell
Interior chapter illustrations by Zachary Woomer
Full Character Illustration (Jack) by Kip Ayers

ISBN 978-0985570910

Library of Congress Control Number: 2014908243

Visit www.jacktaylorcases.com

CNWynn Publications
P.O. Box 328, Cheswold, DE 19936

*Special thanks to my coworkers from here to Kentucky, my family from here to California, and my friends from here to the ones protecting us overseas. I am thankful to repeat the same day with you all.*

*For little Mike, my big brother and an amazing father we all miss very much.*

# Evidence

# The Holiday Hotel

# *Prologue*

Jack awoke slowly to a blinding light above his head. His eyes adjusted with some difficulty, as if he'd been asleep for some time now. He was lying in a bed but couldn't quite remember how he'd gotten there. His arms and legs felt heavy as he struggled to sit up. He could feel the tightly wrapped bandages that held his hair out of his eyes. The steady beeping of a nearby machine and the scuffling of people walking by were the only things he could focus on. He rubbed his eyes but could only make out a few blurry shapes. The window to his left displayed the sun clearly, as if nothing at all were wrong in the world. A television that hung high on the wall in front of his bed was turned off. And on his left, between the window and his bed, was what seemed to be a monitor that was measuring each steady heartbeat. As he turned his head to the right, he noticed a girl who was about his age with long, flowing sun-red hair lying in a similar bed near him. She was not moving.

She appeared to be fairly beaten up—mostly around her arms and head, as they were bandaged up. He could also see some bruising and cuts on her face. As he realized that he was in a hospital, Jack tried to remember what had brought him there or why the girl seemed slightly familiar, but not quite recognizable. She was like a total stranger he had only met once and couldn't bring himself to recall when.

He tried to stand up and walk to the doorway across the room, but a long beep, which he recognized as the sound of a flat-lining heart monitor, stopped him mid-motion. Feeling his chest and arms, he was fairly sure he was alright. Nurses and a doctor came rushing in but stopped suddenly when they noticed he was sitting up.

"Will someone alert his mother? It's not his monitor, but he is awake," the doctor ordered. A male nurse ran from the room, and Jack realized they hadn't had rushed in for him. Two other nurses prepped a crash cart as the doctor prepared to revive the red-haired girl. His eyes fixed upon Jack slightly, as well.

"Jack?!" yelled a woman's voice as she ran into the room. He tried to focus on the girl next to him as they attempted to bring her back.

"Hurry with the cart! We're gonna lose her," the doctor demanded.

"I can't believe you're awake!" said the woman running to him in tears.

"Mom?" Jack asked in a hoarse voice. "You're alive?"

"Clear!" the doctor yelled as he jolted the girl, who was only a few feet away. The room began to spin as Jack felt each shock they gave her bringing back a part of his memory. "Charge it again!" the doctor shouted. "Clear!"

Finally, it all came rushing back to Jack like a flood, and he began to drown in the chaos. . .

# Chapter 1
## Déjà Vu

It was a chilly morning, like most during the winter season. The wind blew hard, rustling the branches of bare trees throughout the neighborhood. Frost stained the windows of cars that lined the steep streets like the dust of white spray paint. There was no snow on the ground, but the dark clouds above looked as if they were debating the urge to allow it. A few stars were left, but they were close to fading completely. The orange glow of the sun against the dark-blue sky slowly peeked above the horizon as if it were waking from a long sleep.

The area was practically empty, except for the widow, Mrs. Johnson. She was a plump, talkative woman with graying red hair who began each morning with a walk around the neighborhood. Her husband had died over six years ago, but she continued their ritual everyday as if he were still alive, jogging beside her with each step she took. As usual, she wore a shiny pink jumpsuit with matching hat and gloves.

After jogging in place, she'd stretch her weary bones, take a few deep breaths, and close her eyes, willing herself to go on. A few steps out of her front yard and she was on her way. The shiny pink fabric reflected the sun's rays brightly as she turned the corner.

In the house across the street, Jack, a thin thirteen-year-old boy with short, curly jet-black hair and pearl-brown eyes, lay awake in his upstairs bedroom. He had a slightly pale complexion, because he spent most of his time inside now. The circles under his eyes were clearly visible after the last few nights of tossing. He continued to wake up, startled by bad dreams and unable to sleep any longer, with a familiar sense of déjà vu that he was unable to place.

His bedroom was still dark; the closed window blinds blocked the light from outside. Clothes littered the floor after he had packed the night before. His surrounding walls were painted sky blue, and a signed poster of his favorite football player hung across from him. Scattered papers, pencils, and school books sat on a desk that stood in the corner.

He awaited the sound of footsteps coming up the stairs, signaling the wakeup call from his mother. He passed a small dark-metallic-green detective's flashlight between his fingers. It was a gift his father had left him the previous year. It was no longer than an unsharpened number-two pencil and slightly wider than a quarter. The handle was inlaid with a magnifying glass, and a bright gold engraving on its side read "Light up the Darkness."

It still reminded him of staying up late with his father on weekends. They would watch old detective shows and crime dramas, trying to solve the mystery before the private investigator could. Jack always had great attention to detail, so did his father — in different ways. It was their favorite way to bond when his father was home from business trips. However, it had been over a year since they had been able to solve a crime together.

Through the magnifying glass of the flashlight, he could see the ceiling fan, unmoving and hovering over his head. He glanced at his dresser, where *The Big Guide to Finding Clues* book that his mother had given him for his birthday lay. It explained how to be a detective, how to find the first clue, and what to look for in a suspect. He had read it so often that the binding was coming apart. Though lately, it had acquired a thin layer of dust from not being moved in many months.

Jack's thumb ran up the side of the flashlight, and, to his shock, the whole room seemed to fill with light, as if the sun had come out from hiding in his closet. He began to rub his eyes to adjust to the brightness and then realized someone had turned his lamp on.

"Jack, are you up yet?" came a woman's voice. "It's time to get ready to leave. Did you sleep alright?"

"Uh yeah, Mom. Just fine. I'm awake," Jack replied. He managed a fake yawn, as if he'd just woken up, and then stashed his flashlight under the pillow, hoping his mother hadn't noticed.

The look on his mother's face resembled the clouds outside, debating with themselves. She had the same jet-black hair her son did, but it came down to her shoulders framing her bronze colored skin and sapphire-blue eyes. She was dressed in black pinstriped pants and a red turtleneck sweater covered her thin neck. Her eyes narrowed sharply the way a mother's does when they know something.

"Jack, are you sure you're feeling well enough to do this today?" She sounded more concerned than she meant to, and Jack immediately became defensive, as if he knew what she was going to say.

"I'm fine, Mom. It's not like it'll get any easier if we keep waiting," Jack answered flatly. "We've been planning it for a month. I'll be okay."

After sitting up, he walked to the bathroom to get ready. His mother watched as he shut the door firmly. Her eyes drifted to the ceiling as she seemed to fill with concern, hoping that today would go smoother than the rest of the month had. Then, looking around the room, she found his packed duffle bag among the shirts and socks on the floor at the foot of his bed and carried it downstairs to place it next to hers.

Once Jack was showered, he put on a pair of black jeans, a blue shirt, and a black leather jacket and then walked downstairs. He passed by photos of himself growing up and one of his parents' wedding day. The Christmas tree downstairs looked the same as every other year's, but looking down at one gift in particular, he knew the spirit just wasn't there. Now it reminded him of things he couldn't change, and that just upset him even more.

Turning the corner to where his mother stood in the kitchen, he watched her staring at something in her hand. When she heard him, she quickly hid it and began serving breakfast. As she wiped her face with her shoulder, it suddenly occurred to Jack that he wasn't the only one hiding things.

"Oh, I almost forgot," Jack said to himself. He ran back upstairs and into his room and grabbed the flashlight under his pillow. Once it was securely in his pocket, he hurried back downstairs and sat at the kitchen table as his mother stood with two plates in her hands.

With an eyebrow raised, she asked him, "What did you forget?"

"I had to get my flashlight," Jack said regrettably.

She sighed. "Is it really necessary to bring that thing everywhere you go? I thought we agreed to move on after today."

"We did agree," Jack said, picking at his scrambled eggs, "but it doesn't mean I have to drop everything. Besides, the day isn't even over yet. It's like we keep going over this . . . ,"

She stared at him with a confused expression but decided not to press the issue. It had already been a stressful beginning; so instead of arguing, they ate breakfast together in silence.

Afterward, they loaded the luggage and prepared themselves for the long drive. Jack's mom warmed up the car and asked Jack to grab the gift for his father from under the tree and to check his room for anything else he might need. He did as he was told, taking the wrapped present addressed to his father and remembering to grab his toothbrush from the bathroom. As he walked back toward the front door to leave, he stopped, turned around, and hurried into the kitchen.

The smells of bacon, eggs, and toast still coursed through the room. He quickly opened the drawer, searching for what she had stashed. After her reaction to his presence, he was fairly sure it wasn't a gift or anything for him. It seemed like she was trying to hide something instead. He rummaged inside the drawer, pulling out oven mitts and pot holders, until he found a tear-stained photo of their family.

Jack looked at himself in the picture, remembering when it was taken. He was no older than nine, sitting between his mother and father. His father smiled happily with his curly, dirty-blond hair. He was wearing his glasses, as usual, hiding his pearl-brown eyes that Jack had been born with as well. They were all dressed in matching green Christmas sweaters. He wiped away a few tears that his mother had left and placed it back in the drawer. Finally, he took a deep breath, took his coat, and joined his mother at the car.

The sun was higher in the sky now, and the remaining dark clouds had started to separate. Some of the frost had begun to melt off the cars on the street, making the windshields look as tearful as the photo in the kitchen.

Jack walked to the passenger side of the car. His mother was waving to Mrs. Johnson, who had finished the second lap of her jog. She was panting as she made her way over to the car, removing her gloves and rubbing her hands together. For as long as he'd been her neighbor, she had walked every morning, waving to him as he went to the bus stop. It occurred to him that as long as she'd been walking daily, it hadn't seemed to make a difference to her figure. The suit she wore was just as stuffed as it always had been.

"Dawn. Jack. Merry Christmas to you both," said Mrs. Johnson. "Leaving out so soon? It's early for you isn't it, Dawn?" Jack's mother started to speak, but Mrs. Johnson was a woman who never had to take a breath. "Who's the lovely gift for?" she asked.

"It's for Jack's father," his mother stated. "Jack wanted to bring him a gift today."

Mrs. Johnson almost spoke, but then looked as if she were on the verge of tears. Jack wondered how her husband had died. Since he'd been married to Mrs. Johnson, Jack assumed talked to death would be a likely answer. It seemed as if she were about to do herself in with a lack of oxygen when suddenly her mouth opened slightly and her eyes watered. "Is it the twenty-first already? I can't believe it's been a month since you moved here. I know how hard it is, especially around the holidays and today being his birthday. I do think of my dear Henry quite often around this time," she sobbed. After a minute of frantic apologizing and remembering her late husband, she finally asked a question that required an answer. "Where are you going to see him?"

Jack spoke up before his mother had a chance to realize Mrs. Johnson's mouth was no longer moving. "We're going to the bay in Maryland for the weekend. It's near my dad's hometown. That's where he was moved to."

Mrs. Johnson looked at Jack and gave him a big hug. As he felt all the air leave his body, it occurred to him that she was a lot stronger than she looked. When she finally released him, he had to check his pockets to be sure his flashlight was still in one piece. Jack's mother made an excuse to get going before traffic got bad. They wished Mrs. Johnson a Merry Christmas, climbed into the car, and waved goodbye to her. Jack sat in the passenger's seat as his mother buckled herself into the driver's seat.

Their eyes met for a moment before she spoke again. "Honey, after this weekend, we have to start discussing what's going on with you, or we won't be able to deal with it later. It's not a good idea to carry this pain with you forever.

And doing things like being late to school because you forgot your flashlight or not showing up at all is not going to make it any better." She looked at him sympathetically. She continued with a sigh, "I just want to help you. It's gonna be hard for me to see him now that he's left us too, honey, but—"

"But it's not your fault he left us, is it?" Jack interrupted. "I pushed him too far last time. I don't see why it's so bad for me to have it with me. When we get there, I just wanna spend as much time with him that I can. So, can we please go?"

She stared at him as he looked out his window. "Jack, these things just happen. There was nothing you could do to stop it."

"Mom, just let it go, please," Jack said softly, looking through the side window.

She wasn't sure what else she could say. She knew nothing would help the situation, and that made it more frustrating to not be able to help her son. So instead, she slowly put the car into drive and pulled out of the driveway.

Making their way down the road, they drove out of the neighborhood in silence. Jack peered out the window as they passed the school he went to. Shame started to creep in as he thought about what he had said to his mother and how much this was affecting her, as well. Yet his mind was too occupied, and he felt weary of how often they seemed to have the same conversation.

As the day went on, more and more cars joined theirs on the road. Like packs of animals smelling meat for the first time, people hurried from store to store for gifts, holiday foods, and everything in between. Except for a stop at a restaurant, hours passed before Jack or his mother spoke. It was awkwardly quiet, except for the occasional car roaring by, the voice of the GPS unit giving directions, or the sound of the radio playing random carols that made Jack feel anything but cheerful.

He still couldn't shake the feeling that he'd been down this road recently. From the cars going by with out-of-state plates to the people waiting at the bus stop, they all looked strangely familiar—almost like a dream he'd just woken up from that lingered in the back of his mind. Even a kid who looked excitedly through a store window and pointed at a toy gave Jack the feeling he'd seen it before. But it wasn't until he noticed a department store's Santa chasing his hat down the sidewalk that he broke the silence and asked his mother about it.

"Um, Mom?" he questioned hesitantly, "Have we been through this city recently?"

She made a right turn back on to the highway as the GPS directed before answering. "No, I don't think so. . . . It's probably been about six months since we came through here last. We came to visit your aunt Linda in Westchester, I think. Why?" She glanced to her right to make sure he was alright, but he only continued to think hard. She couldn't help wondering if there was something else going on with him that he wouldn't divulge.

Jack didn't like her to worry about him, especially since he wasn't sure himself what was wrong. So he looked back to his mother and did his best to be nonchalant. "No reason. I just . . ." He tried to quickly think of a reason to change the subject. "I need to use the bathroom."

"Oh, okay. We can pull in somewhere," she replied, keying in restroom on the GPS unit as she took the next exit.

They were directed a few miles down the road to a small rest area. Jack took out his flashlight to pass the time and began looking through the handle again. Now that it was almost noon, the sun came in through the windows, brightening the gold engraving even more. Through the windshield, he could easily see farther down the road with the magnified handle. Taking notice of a few trees with almost no leaves, an old, dilapidated out-of-place building, and a few large utility trucks parked farther down, he could almost make out the rest area.

Jack witnessed something shiny come streaking down through the air and land on the road directly in the pathway of the moving vehicle. Before he could register what it was, there was a loud pop, like the sound of a gunshot hitting the car, forcing them to pull over. They found themselves on the side of the road about a half mile away from the rest area. Exiting the car carefully, Jack and his mother checked themselves and then stepped to the side of the car.

"Watch out for the traffic," she warned him. "Too many people get into accidents just stepping onto the road. I don't want you getting hurt." They looked on the driver's side and realized the front tire had blown. Jack wondered if he should tell her what he had glimpsed falling from the sky. However, looking all over the black road and again at the tire, he couldn't find anything on the ground that could have punctured it—no small pieces of metal or anything sharp at all.

*Where was it*, he thought to himself. He began to wonder if he had imagined it all. Maybe the tire simply blew. Either way, it seemed better to not mention it.

Deciding to walk to the rest area, Jack left his mother as she continued to the nearest auto shop to replace the damaged tire. He surveyed the small town across from the rest stop as he walked, taking notice of the buildings and trees he'd seen through his flashlight handle. Close up, the old abandoned building he'd seen earlier seemed much more out of place than the others. The other buildings appeared new and lively in comparison.

Before he realized, it was late in the afternoon when he arrived at the rest area. The sun was shining brighter, and the clouds were almost nonexistent. But the cold was unmistakable. Wind blew from all directions with such a force that he struggled to keep his coat closed. Even the buildings creaked in protest of the harsh winds as it appeared to be bending away from its force.

The rest area had a strong resemblance to a ranch-style building. Its gray stone walls were surrounded by a green field, like a small national park. Huge freightliners parked next to each other as tourists walked around, taking pictures of the winter scenery. The cold became bitter as the wind blew harder. After a while, even the tourists were running in to warm up.

Once inside, Jack used the restroom. Then he decided to wait a few minutes for the winds to calm before heading back out. Passing by a gift shop with snow globes and a small convenience area, he wandered around to the south side of the rest stop, where information about the town's history was displayed. Facts and photos about the buildings were displayed on most of the walls. One photo in particular tugged at his attention; it was of the same old building across the street. He didn't think that the photo appeared to be old enough to be on the wall of historical buildings. The display didn't even say what type of building it was, and there wasn't much information about it—not even a date. Only the faded name of the company that had designed it appeared on the display, but even that was too difficult to read. Jack decided to take a better look at the building, so he headed outside.

The wind had finally calmed since he'd arrived, and more people began showing up. The rest area was now bustling with truckers and tourist families. He carried on outside, passing by two strangers who debated if they had met each other before, and looked around at the few buildings in his view. A busy coffee shop bustling with people sat next to a newspaper stand. Next to that was an alley. The abandoned building from the photo stood just beyond the alley.

He hadn't noticed as much of it from across the road when he had walked by before with the rushing vehicles going by. The building seemed to have aged over a hundred years more than the other buildings in the photograph. It was one story high and had peeling stones all around it. The windows were boarded up, and from such a distance, they were too dark to see into, like it had once been filled with smoke that was never released. Two gargoyles with menacing grins stood guard on either side of the stairwell. The french doors at the top of the stairs had been trimmed with some kind of metal that was now rusting.

He noticed a hanging sign, but it was too far away to for him to read what was written on it. It continued to catch his eye as he walked by, and although his flashlight lens was made to magnify, he thought it may be powerful enough to make out a few letters. Looking through the lens, he could almost make out the word *foreclosed* written on it. But besides that, there were no other distinctive details to the building. He wasn't sure if it was once an office or a retail store. Yet there was something unusually telling attached to the building. A shining golden plaque with engravings was bolted on the right side of the building.

Jack was wondering how something so new would continue to be as pristine on a building in such bad shape when a small gap appeared between the doors, as if they were opening. He began to walk toward the road until he ran into the path of a young girl and was knocked down.

"Oh, I'm sorry. I didn't expect you to be here. Are you okay?" asked the girl. She reached out her hand to help Jack up.

"Yeah, I'm fine. Don't worry about it," Jack said, a bit embarrassed. He hadn't realized how surprised she actually was until he was standing up again and able to look at her properly. She was slightly taller than him, and she was wearing blue jeans that were stained with various colors of ink. She also wore a black shirt under a clean white peacoat. Her short blond hair was hidden under a pink-and-white knit hat. The sun's reflection in her green eyes made her pupils look like sunflowers in a grassy field. Small cuts covered her slender hands, and she spoke properly, as if she were actually much older than she appeared. But what he noticed most was that she had the same expression Mrs. Johnson had given him right before she'd hugged him earlier.

"You weren't here before?" she said quietly with a curious smile, "Who are you?"

Jack wondered what she meant, but he decided not to question it. "Um, my name's Jack. I'm on my way to Maryland with my mom," he said hesitantly.

"Well, it's very nice to meet you. My name is Sonny. I live about two blocks over," she said, pointing a finger with quite a few more cuts to the street farther down. "So why are you going to Maryland?"

It was the same question he'd been asked a hundred times in a hundred different ways like "Where's your dad?" or "When will you see him again?" He sighed.

"Well, we just drove six hours from Michigan, but got a flat tire down the road. We're on our way to visit my dad near the bay. It's where we moved from, so he's back there now." He tried his best to not sound as sullen as he felt. He really didn't want her to feel sorry for him. The sympathy people gave him grew tiresome after a while. But when he glanced up, he noticed her face hadn't changed. She looked neither bored nor remorseful. Her expression was understanding.

"My parents divorced when I was much younger, so I don't see my mother very much since she moved away," she said, walking around Jack as if she were examining him. "It's not easy with just one parent. I used to spend a lot of summers with my Grandmum El and Granddad He, until he passed away."

"Wait," Jack interrupted as she paused in front of him. "Their names were El and He?"

She stopped and smirked, and then she resumed her walk. "Sort of. When I was little I couldn't pronounce their full names, and it just stuck. Well, after my mother left, my Granddad always told me not to dwell or forget the people who are gone, but to keep the memories and appreciate the ones who stay with you. . . . You're worried about seeing him, aren't you?" Sonny asked. "I can tell you were close to him."

Sonny seemed more upbeat than Jack would have thought possible after having your mother leave you. He wasn't sure if he should ask about her father, so he decided not to.

"You think about him a lot don't you?" Sonny asked.

"Yeah, I do all the time," Jack answered, getting lost in his thoughts. "Especially around buildings I haven't seen before. He was an architect. Very detailed oriented in his work."

"Oh, really? Is your plan to follow in his footsteps?" she asked.

"No, it's not for me. I'm not really sure what I want to do anymore," Jack replied, unsure why she was so interested in his life. It was weird for him to talk to his mother about anything; he wasn't sure how much he wanted to tell a stranger. "Before, I wanted to be a detective, but now . . . it seems more like fantasy. I was always more interested in solving puzzles than building. The first building I remember my dad designing was a station for the police department. We spent a lot of time with the officers, and once the building was finished, I knew it would be the best way I could help people."

Just then, the wind picked up again. As Jack turned his head to shield his face, he noticed his mother walking up to them carrying his father's gift and their bags. "I better get going. My mom's on her way," he said to Sonny.

"Okay. Try not to get anymore flat tires." She chuckled.

Jack's curiosity got the better of him, and he called out to her, "Hey, what exactly did you mean earlier about me not being here before?"

She turned around but continued walking backward toward her house. She put her hands into her front pockets and brought out a notepad and red pen and began writing. "If I see you tomorrow, I'll let you know," she replied, placing the items back into her pockets. Then, as quickly as she had appeared, she was gone.

"Who was that, honey?" Jack's mother handed his duffle bag to him.

"Some girl I sort of ran into," he said cautiously. Recognizing the look his mother was giving him, he decided to shrug it off and change the subject. "So what's going on with the car?"

"Well, the attendant at Fast Wheels towed it to the shop but said they'd have to order the right-size tire. It won't be here until tomorrow," she said, looking frustrated with herself. "I completely forgot to put the spare back in after last time. So we'll have to get a room for the night," she continued.

He looked at her unexpectedly, as if the lights in his room had just turned on again. "Really? We're staying in town for the night? What about Dad?"

"We'll just have to get up early and drive the rest of the way tomorrow, instead. It's about a half day's travel to Annapolis," she said, as if preparing for his disappointment.

"I guess," Jack said quietly, unsure if he was glad or disappointed about the delay. He tried not to sound too upset. It occurred to him how coincidental it was that he may actually see Sonny again, but as the wind began to get rougher, the thought quickly left his mind.

His mother seemed satisfied that he hadn't put up a fight about staying the night. They called a taxi to take them to a hotel. The taxi that arrived was the usual yellow-and-black car that Jack had seen in movies, but having never experienced one personally, he didn't realize how small their backseats actually were. As they passed by cars, he felt every turn. As he drove, the driver spouted facts as if he worked for the tourist bureau at the rest stop. Jack could tell from the way the man spoke about the area that he had been here all his life. The missing wedding ring that had left a tan on his finger implied that when he was married, he didn't get to speak much and was making up for it now. However, Jack wasn't paying much attention until the driver mentioned the buildings they were passing. He spoke about the bakery that was turned into a café and the newsstand that had been there for years. Jack thought he would mention the abandoned building next, but he continued past as if it didn't exist.

It wasn't long before the car stopped. The driver told them the total and, once paid, headed back into traffic. They had been dropped off at the Blue Mountain Hotel, a tall building with blue roofs and surrounding tan stones. The sliding-glass doors led to a large open room with a warm fire that increased the already-pleasant atmosphere. A large Christmas tree lightly decorated with white and blue bulbs sat in the corner, and a red bow was delicately placed under the welcome sign at the front desk.

By the time they were settled in their room, had unpacked their bags, and had explored the hotel, the sun had begun to set. Their room was standard, with two queen-sized beds decorated to match the hotel's colors of blue and white. A large window created a beautiful view from the fourth floor that overlooked the town.

Jack unpacked his bag and placed a framed photo of himself with his mother and father and a few friends on the nightstand next to his bed. In the photo, it was summer and they were all near a pool. His two best friends were on each side of him, and his parents were laughing. He hadn't seen his friends since they'd moved, and he couldn't remember smiling like that in a long time.

It was still early in the evening, but he felt a strong urge to go to sleep. His mind was flooding with thoughts. He sat in bed, playing with a deck of cards, tossing them easily into the small opening of a suitcase with a flick of his wrist, as he thought about the strange events that happened in such a short period of time. He thought of the mysterious girl and wondered what he was going to say when he finally got to see his father. Under normal circumstances, he wouldn't have thought twice about what had happened. Almost every romance movie he'd ever tried to avoid included a passing of two strangers who bump into each other. Besides, it wasn't the best time for him to make friends. Usually, he just wanted to be alone, or maybe he was just used to it. It plagued him for a while, until his mother asked about dinner.

"You know, you're pretty good at that," his mother said, watching him land two cards into the trash at once. "So what do you feel like tonight? Pizza or Chinese takeout?"

"Huh? Sorry. I wasn't paying attention," Jack replied, setting the rest of the deck down. "Yeah, pizza's fine?" Jack replied, only half listening.

When it arrived, they watched a movie and ate together, sitting on the bed. Nightfall came. Through the window, Jack could see all the Christmas lights that lit the city. It was like watching all of the stars in the universe from a closer view. The combination of peacefulness and pizza made him tired. So he told his mother goodnight and climbed into the warm bed, watching the picture on his nightstand. His eyelids got heavier as he thought about going to the bay the next day. In an instant, he was asleep.

That night, Jack's dream was just as odd as the rest of the day had been. In his dream, it was very cold, and a thick layer of snow covered everything in sight. He dragged a present for his father to a large body of water, ready to dump it. The present was three times its original size and incredibly heavy, and it seemed to get larger and heavier the closer he got to the water. No one else was around, not his mother or passersby. There were no birds on ledges or any animals anywhere in sight. The area was completely still, as though the world had ended and he were the only survivor.

A voice croaked through the silence. It was very close, but he couldn't see anyone.

"How can you let me go so easily? Do I not matter?"

Jack looked down at his hands as they vibrated with the voice. It was coming from inside the box. The ground stirred slowly beneath him as it spoke again.

"Is it so easy to let go? It's your fault we're apart! You should be apart!"

The voice inside the box was causing the earth to shake violently. The ground began to crumble away, revealing an endless black space underneath Jack. Debris thrashed everywhere as he began to choke on falling dust that was swallowed by the darkness. He attempted to grab on to something—or anything at all. But, before long, gravity took over and he plummeted. Then there was nothingness. . . .

The small glowing hand of a young girl reached out to him. The hand came from an arm in a white peacoat. Her slender fingers were no longer covered in cuts, and her jeans were no longer stained with ink. He was sure it was Sonny, but her hair was much longer and fiery red. Looking into her rainbow-colored eyes was like looking into a prism. As her fingers grasped his, his descent slowed, and he began to return to the surface. She had no problem lifting him, as if he weighed nothing at all. Jack panicked as he realized that she wasn't attached to anything but simply floated upward, back onto the ground.

Solid surface met their feet. Sonny presented a small box wrapped in red paper and green bow to him. He cautiously took it from her as she motioned to open it. But before he did, he already knew what was inside, remembering the wrapping being the same as before. Slowly, he ripped the paper apart and removed the lid, looking into the box beneath. Jack reached his hand inside and pulled out the same gift his father had left him the previous Christmas—the small green flashlight with magnifying-glass-inlaid handle.

Jack stared at the girl with uncertainty and asked her if she was, in fact, Sonny. But as his lips formed the words, nothing came out. She pointed down the street. His mouth fell wide open, stunned. He hurriedly put his flashlight's handle up to his eye and stared through the glass magnifying piece. Through it, he could clearly see the foreclosed sign, the gargoyle statues, and boarded-up windows on an old dilapidated building. He couldn't understand how it was possible for a building to move to another location. Yet, here was the same building with french doors that was across from the rest area. It was surrounded by different buildings but just as out of place. The sparkling trail a few yards away leading to the front doors stood out the most. The trail was made of gold dust, but when he lowered the flashlight, the trail disappeared.

He brought the magnifying glass up to his eye and then pulled it away, watching the trail appear and disappear repeatedly until he finally looked at the girl in confusion and formed the silent question, "What does this mean?"

As she spoke to him, the words rang in a loud but muffled voice.

"Light up the darkness," she seemed to say.

"What'd you say?" Jack asked, his voice returning as he strained to hear her clearly.

She spoke again. "Light up yet?" It sounded as if two people were speaking, and the words became less muffled.

"I can't understand you," he said, even more confused. His voice had completely returned.

"Jack, are you up yet?" called his mother's voice clearly as she began to shake him.

Jack awoke holding the flashlight in his hand, as if he'd been holding it the entire time. He found himself staring through the magnifying glass handle that was pointed up at the ceiling. Something seemed out of place as he stared at a ceiling fan. Although he was in a familiar setting, he was unsure how he'd gotten there.

"It's time to get ready to leave. Did you sleep alright?" she asked.

As he rubbed his eyes, he surveyed the room, expecting a different environment. Instead of the blue-and-white surroundings of the hotel room, he found himself looking at a poster of his favorite football player, *The Big Guide to Finding Clues* on his dresser with the thin layer of dust, and his packed duffle bag sitting at the foot of his bed. His heart beat faster.

Jack's face turned to an even paler shade of white as he leaped out of bed, dropping his flashlight onto the floor. He ran to the window and waited a few moments. His mother watched in complete bewilderment as he stared through the open blinds at the frost-covered cars until he saw her. Mrs. Johnson was making her lap around the neighborhood in the same reflective-pink jumpsuit as before. His confusion was unyielding as he slowly turned around and answered his mother the same way he was sure he had the day before.

"Uh yeah, Mom. Just fine," he lied. "I'm awake." This morning, his ominous, vague feelings of déjà vu were replaced with absolute certainty.

# Chapter 2
## Midnight Meeting

It was the same chilly morning, once again; the stars weren't completely faded, and the wind blew fairly hard. Mrs. Johnson, wearing her shiny pink jumpsuit with matching gloves and hat, was on her first lap around the block, just the same. The early morning sun reflected off the pink fibers of the suit.

Jack wasn't sure what to think. His mother stood watching him steadily. When he got up, she asked, "Jack, are you sure you're feeling well enough to do this today?" She was dressed exactly the same as before—black pinstriped pants and a red turtleneck sweater.

"Yeah, Mom," Jack replied as he sat in his bed, wondering how she was keeping her composure about this so much better than he was. Acting like this was a normal situation was weird enough for her, but now he was just lost about what was going on. He looked around the room and then asked, "Didn't we do this yesterday?"

"Yesterday?" she asked. "Do what yesterday?" Her concern was obviously growing. "Did something happen at school?"

"The hotel room and the flat tire? Going to the bay?" he asked, hoping this was all some kind of joke. He'd prefer that to appearing crazy.

"Well, honey, you know we're going there today. Is that what this all about? Did you have a bad dream about visiting him?" she asked, appearing a little relieved that he was actually discussing his father.

"Right, I guess it was a dream," Jack said, puzzled. He was plagued by the question of why she couldn't remember the day before but he could. Jack found it almost annoying. But he began to think that maybe, somehow, he'd just had a premonition, or maybe something strange had happened to his mother to erase her memory. Either way, it was early in the morning, and thinking about it so much made his head hurt. "I'm going to take a shower and get ready," he stated finally.

Her eyes drifted to the ceiling as she seemed to fill with concern and hope that today would go smoother than the rest of the month had gone. Then, looking around the room, she found his duffle bag among the shirts and socks on the floor. It sat at the foot of his bed, already packed. She carried it downstairs to place it next to hers.

After Jack was dressed in his blue shirt, black jeans, and black leather jacket, he headed downstairs. However, this time he remembered to run back up to get his flashlight before he reached the bottom of the stairs. Strangely, even after searching the floor, he didn't see it anywhere. After searching through clothes spread on the floor, an idea developed, and he checked under his pillow. He was sure he hadn't hidden it this time, but there it lay, just as it had the day before. He thought for a moment, reassuring himself that his mother couldn't have known where he'd hid it before and that she wouldn't have bothered to hide it today. Things weren't making sense, but Jack continued on cautiously, wondering who had replaced it under his pillow.

Once the flashlight was in his pocket, Jack hurried back downstairs, turned the corner, and sat at the kitchen table. His mother stood with two plates in her hands. Even breakfast looked the same.

"What did you forget?" she asked.

He looked at her, puzzled. "How did you know I forgot something?"

"You just walked downstairs and said you forgot something, and then ran back upstairs," she replied.

Jack's head began to hurt even more. "Yeah, my flashlight. But I didn't . . . ," he faltered.

She sighed. "Is it really necessary to bring that thing everywhere you go? I thought we agreed to move on after today."

"Mom, this is getting really confusing," Jack said, holding his head. "We did agree, but it doesn't mean I have to drop everything. It's like we . . . keep going over this?" Jack hesitated. The words were leaving his mouth without him thinking about it, and he wondered if this all had happened even before yesterday. She looked at him with a confused expression, but she didn't press the issue. Instead, they ate breakfast together in silence.

Afterward, they loaded the luggage and prepared themselves for the long drive. Jack's mom warmed up the car while Jack walked back into the house to get his toothbrush and father's gift before she had even asked. The smells of bacon, eggs, and toast still coursed through the room. He walked back into the kitchen first, to see if the photo was there. He opened the drawer. As he expected, under oven mitts and potholders was the picture of both of his parents with him sitting between them. In a tear-stained photo that his mother had left, they all wore matching green Christmas sweaters. When the items were placed back over the photo, he closed the drawer. Then he grabbed his toothbrush and his father's gift; he took a deep breath and headed back outside.

The sun was up, shining fully now, and the dark clouds that were left had started to separate. Jack walked to the passenger side of the car as his mother was waving to Mrs. Johnson, who had finished her second lap. She was panting as she made her way over to the car, removing her gloves and rubbing her hands together. Jack's hopes increased when she appeared. He had a glimmer of hope that she, like him, knew that the day was repeating itself and that maybe it was just his mother who didn't realize. It was possible that his mom had somehow been brainwashed. However, as Mrs. Johnson greeted them just as identically as before, he was instantly disappointed.

"Dawn. Jack. Merry Christmas to you both," said Mrs. Johnson. "Leaving out so soon? It's early for you isn't it, Dawn?" Jack's mother started to speak, but Mrs. Johnson, once again, went uninterrupted. "Who's the lovely gift for?" she asked.

"It's for Jack's father," his mother stated. "Jack wanted to bring him a gift today."

Mrs. Johnson tried to speak but then looked as if she were on the verge of tears. Jack was wondering if there was something he could do or not do to make things change, when suddenly Mrs. Johnson's mouth opened slightly and her eyes watered.

"Is it the twenty-first already? I can't believe it's been a month since you moved here. I know how hard it is, especially around the holidays and today being his birthday. I do think of my dear Henry quite often around this time," she sobbed. After a minute of frantic apologizing and remembering her late husband, she finally asked a question that required an answer. "Where are you going to see him?"

Jack waited, wondering if his mom would speak up this time, but she glared at him, instead. "Well, answer her, Jack," she said, looking thoroughly irritated.

Jack hoped that he could change this small event and that someone would realize this had all been done before. Appearing defeated, he did as his mother instructed and replied, "We're going to the bay in Maryland for the weekend. It's near my dad's hometown."

Mrs. Johnson looked at Jack, and he braced himself as she gave him a big hug. He felt all the air leave his body as he waited for her to let go. Jack's mother made an excuse to get going before traffic got bad. They wished Mrs. Johnson a Merry Christmas and climbed inside the car.

Jack sat in the passenger's seat as his mom sat in the driver's seat. After the same discussion they'd had before, she slowly put the car into drive and pulled out of the driveway. They made their way down the road, riding in silence all over again.

Jack peered out the window as they passed by the school he went to. He told himself that there must be a reason why all this was happening. That's when he remembered Sonny and what she had said: "If I see you tomorrow, I'll let you know."

The feeling of possibly not being alone in this made him more anxious as they drove farther and farther from their house. At that point, all he could do was hope that she would be there and that maybe she might remember him.

It wasn't until they had been on the road for a while that he thought about the dream he'd had. He envisioned the red-haired girl with rainbow eyes who had rescued him from falling and recalled how his father's gift had become so massive in size and weight. However, the part that haunted him the most was the voice that had come from the box. He could almost feel it shaking his hands now as he stared at the gift, as if it had really happened.

As the day went on, more and more cars came onto the road, just as before. People hurried from stores, rushing to buy gifts. Hours passed, and no one in the car spoke. It was awkwardly quiet. Only the occasional car roaring by, the voice of the GPS unit giving directions, or the sound of the radio playing random carols broke the silence.

They passed by the same people waiting at the bus stop and the kid who pointed excitedly while he looked through a store window. Then they passed the department store's Santa chasing his hat down the sidewalk. Jack's mom made a right turn back on to the highway as the GPS directed. As they drove, Jack felt uneasy. He couldn't understand why at first, but as they drove along, he began to feel spots of his mind ease away what had happened yesterday. He started to forget the hotel room and the flat tire. The farther they traveled, the more details he began to forget of the blond girl he'd run into.

*Or was she a brunette?* he asked himself. As they proceeded, he began to forget what she'd worn, what she'd said, and her name. *Sandy or Bunny,* he thought as they passed by a mattress store building with a large sign reading "Best Rest Beds." A nagging feeling of something important that he couldn't remember crept into the back of Jack's mind like a spider creeping into a web, until finally. . . . "Wait, Mom, I think I have to use the bathroom," Jack remembered as they were very close to passing the exit.

"Oh, okay. We can pull in somewhere," she replied, keying in restroom on the GPS unit. After she turned off the next exit, they were directed a couple of miles down the road to the rest area.

Jack felt relieved as he could suddenly remember Sonny in vivid description. He stared out the car's front window, wondering why, of all the things that had happened this morning, this detour almost hadn't. As they got closer to the trees with hardly any leaves and the old, dilapidated building, Jack waited for the shining streak. With the building in sight, Jack watched the road closely. He hoped maybe the flat tire had something to do with it, but he couldn't see anything shiny coming down from the sky.

He braced himself, hoping something would happen, causing them to stop. He closed his eyes, and the car was quiet. Finally, he heard a sound like a pin drop. Readying himself, he smiled, feeling content that this one event he wanted to continue hadn't changed.

*POP!*

They were forced to pull over on the side of the road a half mile from the rest area. They checked each other and stepped outside of the car.

"Watch out for the traffic," Jack's mother warned him. "Too many people get into accidents just stepping onto the road. I don't want you getting hurt."

Jack didn't even bother looking at the tire this time. Instead, he waited for the moment when his mother would go to the auto shop and he could go to the rest area. He began to feel nervous. What if the girl didn't remember him? What if it all happened again tomorrow? Worst of all, what if he was stuck in an endless loop for the rest of his life and he would never make it to his father?

It was late in the afternoon before he made it to the rest area. The sun was shining brighter, and the clouds were almost nonexistent, but the cold was piercing. Wind blew from all directions with such force; he was struggling to keep his coat closed, but he was determined to make it to the building. Buildings creaked against the harsh wind as he passed them. The abandoned building seemed to follow his movement as he passed it.

As he approached the rest area, the air became warm, as if it were an old friend greeting him. The gray stone ranch-style design surrounded by a green field felt just as sheltering inside as it had before. The information on display remained unchanged. Even the photo of the building he couldn't stop studying still plagued him. The lack of details made him uneasy, as if something unnatural had happened there.

Once inside, he used the restroom and waited for the wind to calm so he could make his way back out. More people showed up, and the rest area was now bustling with truckers and tourist families. He continued outside, ready to wait for the bump into Sonny, hoping she would be waiting for him, too.

Jack paused across the street from the old dilapidated building, watching its peeling stones and dark boarded-up windows. Then, just as before, as if asking him to enter, the gap between the french doors appeared. It seemed even wider now, as if it were motioning him to enter. Part of him wanted to run across the street to it, but he knew he needed to wait for the girl to arrive. So he braced himself, expecting the bump that would signal her presence, but it didn't come. He looked to his left, the direction she had come from before, but he didn't see her. Then, to his right, he spotted what looked like the back of her blond hair tucked into a pink–and–white knit hat. Somehow, she had completely bypassed him and he hadn't noticed.

Jack wasn't sure if this was good or not. It was a change, but not the one he'd hoped for. He ran after her and tapped her on the shoulder, unsure how he should approach and not knowing if she would run away if he sounded delusional. Since this was the first thing that happened differently today, he urged himself to attempt something.

"Excuse me?" he said, waiting for her to acknowledge him.

It was definitely the same girl with the pink-and-white knit hat covering most of her blond hair, except she wasn't wearing a coat, just a white-and-pink t-shirt with a few ink stains. She was also wearing different ink-covered blue jeans with a notepad in the back pocket. Jack wondered how she wasn't freezing, but the thought quickly left his mind when she asked, "Can I help you?" She glared at Jack uncertainly.

He began to think that she didn't remember him, and he wondered how to proceed. "Um, don't I know you?" he asked nervously.

She waited a moment before answering. "Maybe, you do look familiar, but you'll have to refresh my memory."

Jack doubted himself a little, wondering if this was some kind of code or if she really didn't recognize him. Yesterday, he couldn't get her to stop talking to him, but today she didn't seem as interested. Her face was unchanged, which wasn't helping him. So after debating silently with himself, he decided that sounding crazy and knowing was worth the risk.

"Your name is Sonny? And you told me yesterday if I saw you today, you'd tell me what you meant about . . . not seeing me before?"

Even as he said it, he knew it sounded strange. It was confusing enough yesterday, and she looked as if she were about to run when her eyes widened. Jack tried frantically to think of a good excuse to get out of the situation.

*Maybe her name isn't Sonny,* he thought. *The girl yesterday was wearing a coat, so why isn't this one?* He waited for her to turn and run, but she waited, as if she were looking through him, for several seconds. Finally, she took his hand and whispered, "Follow me quickly and be sure not to say anything."

Under normal circumstances, it's always good advice to not follow strangers, but these were obviously not normal circumstances. At this point, since no one else appeared able to help him, Jack accompanied Sonny as she led him by the hand. They walked quickly behind the rest area. Sonny looked in every direction, as if making sure no one was around, before speaking again. At that instant, Jack wouldn't have been surprised if she'd told him she was a secret agent being monitored at all times. When she did speak, he tried his best to be prepared for anything.

~ 35 ~

"Every day I wake up, and it's been the same day—December twenty-first. Is that happening to you as well?" she asked, speaking quickly.

Jack nodded; he was in too much shock to speak. She was talking fast like Mrs. Johnson, but in short bursts. He hung on to her every word, hoping she might have the answers he'd been looking for.

Sonny continued, "I still haven't figured out why, but I think you and I are the only ones that know. Anyone else I asked about it acted like I was crazy. At one point, I began thinking I really was crazy, too. So I just stayed quiet and didn't talk about it anymore, to anyone."

"You're not crazy," Jack piped up, suddenly regaining his ability to communicate.

She smiled. "I really wasn't sure what to do before we met yesterday. I thought I may be dreaming after all these days alone."

At that moment, Jack remembered the question he'd had the day before. "What did you mean yesterday about not seeing me before, anyways?"

"Well, I was hoping you would understand, since you were the first unusual occurrence I've had since the days began repeating," she said flatly, as if the repeating days weren't unusual already. "Wait, exactly how many days have you known this has been happening?"

Jack thought about it. "Yesterday was the first time. It felt like I had done certain things before, but I didn't remember it like I did today. So, two days, I guess."

"Only two days?!" she asked. Jack wasn't sure if she was confused or just unimpressed, as if it weren't strange enough for her to be bothered with. "I noticed days before then, and I didn't see you until yesterday. The day I ran into you something must have changed. How is that possible?" She was now talking more to herself than to Jack.

"I did see a shiny piece of metal fall on the road that I couldn't find afterwards, but I didn't see it fall today. I can't understand why, but the tire still popped. Might have been a pin or something, but I'm pretty sure it's the reason we got a flat tire. It made this sound like . . . ," Jack's voice trailed off. He was looking at Sonny and wondering what she was thinking about. She was turned away from him, so he wasn't sure if she was even listening.

"Your mom got a flat tire," she repeated as if stating a fact.

"Yeah," he replied. "That's why we stopped here. She's probably on her way back now. I told her I had to use the bathroom, then that thing came through the air."

"That has to be what changed. I don't quite understand why it has only now happened, but it must be why you stopped here." She removed the notepad and a fancy red-and-silver pen from her back pocket and began scribbling frantically. "You will have to figure out where that shiny piece came from. It may be the source of all this that's happening."

A year ago, this would have been the type of thing Jack would jump at, but even this was more than he was used to. "I'm still trying to figure out why we're the only ones that know this is happening," Jack stated quickly, knowing his mother was going to be looking for him soon.

Sonny clicked her pen a few times and spoke hastily. "Well, I have hopes if we find an answer to one, we may find out the other." She glanced up at the clouds. "You should get going. I've been getting better at judging the time between events so no one gets suspicious." She watched Jack and smiled. "That first day I realized days were the same and no one else had was not a particularly good feeling to have alone. I'm glad that we bumped into each other."

Jack hoped it was too cold to see him blushing. "You do seem like you know more about what's going on than I do." He tried to sound more assured than he really was.

They walked back to the front of the rest area, where Sonny would leave him across from the old building they had met in front of.

"Well, my grandfather used to tell me stories of his travels. And, ever since, I always planned to be an investigative journalist and do the same. This could be the perfect story for me."

"Is that where all those cuts came from?" Jack asked as they reached the sidewalk.

She looked down at her hands; it looked as if she'd gotten another one recently. "Paper cuts," she said, shaking her hand from the sting. "Sometimes doing what you love hurts. Whatever's going on might reignite your will to be a detective, too. I'm curious just how smart you might be. Tomorrow we should meet behind the rest area. Be sure to watch the direction of that shiny piece and where it comes from."

Sonny continued walking toward her house. In his mind, Jack ran through everything they had discussed between yesterday and today, and then he called out. "Hey, how long have you . . . been doing this?" he asked, trying to be discreet, so none of the tourists would question it.

She paused and thought for a moment. Looking slightly depressed, she responded, "So far, today is my eighth day." She shrugged. "Hope I see you tomorrow." Then, once again, as quickly as she had appeared, she rounded a corner and was gone.

Slightly astonished about what had just happened, Jack stood and stared at the sidewalk, unable to believe she had gone through what was definitely the most unusual day he had ever had eight times now. Then it occurred to him what day it would be, and he wondered if that meant he had technically missed Christmas. He worried that he had missed his chance to give the gift to his father.

"Who was that, honey?" Jack's mother asked, holding his duffle bag across her shoulder and trailing her bag behind her. He hadn't even realized she was walking up until she spoke.

"Some girl I . . . " He hesitated. "Just met, err, ran into," he corrected. Jack tried to make sure the rest of the night mirrored the night before as much as possible. He even pretended not to hear his mother's question about dinner, which wasn't too difficult, considering that the recent events distracted him anyway. All night, he thought really hard about where the shining streak had come from. It wasn't until he fell asleep, staring at the framed photo from the previous summer again, that anything really different happened that night.

In his dream, it was nightfall and still very cold, like before. However, Jack was in the middle of the rest-area field with a brightly lit podium in front of him. Across from him were two tall covered cages on top of pedestals under a spotlight. To his right sat a group of people on stadium-style bench seats. They resembled the tourist families he had seen earlier. On his right sat another group on benches, but they weren't tourists. They looked like some of the people who were waiting for the bus that they had passed while driving that day. Both sides were lit, so they could all see each other. But their focus was strictly on Jack.

He thought it was some kind of court hearing until he heard someone speak. As the person walked out from the shadows in front of Jack and between the two cages, all the eyes switched to him. He was a tall, handsome man with a sparkling white smile, silvery-white hair, and a blue suit that matched his eyes. Music began from nowhere, and when the man spoke, his voice rang loudly throughout the entire field, as if he had been connected to a loudspeaker.

"Welcome to the greatest game show in your dreams. This is . . . Choose Your Fate!" the man said as he was greeted with applause from the people on the benches. "I'm your host, Ted Thompson, and today we'll be playing for big prizes. Tonight our contestant is a thirteen-year-old boy who has aspirations of being a detective and an obvious thing for blondes. Please welcome Jackson Eli Taylor, Junior." Applause broke out again. "Jack, how do you feel?"

He wasn't exactly sure what was going on or what to say, so he just blurted something out. "Um kinda cold. . . . And I don't have a thing for blondes!"

"Isn't that wonderful, folks," said Ted as the crowd applauded. "Well, let's get started, shall we? Question number one, Jack — what is in the first cage?"

Jack wasn't sure how he had ended up on a game show. As he awaited the first question, the host peered back at him, waiting for an answer. Jack realized the first question had already been asked. He tried to look past all the darkness and into the cage, but he couldn't see anything. With the coverings on top, there was no way he could know. Before he could even take a guess, there was a loud, annoying buzzer.

*Beeeeep!*

~ 40 ~

"Ooh, that's really too bad. Let's show Jack what's in the first cage, shall we, folks," the host said loudly as a light flashed on and flooded the area around the cage with light. The covering fell from the cage. Inside, on the ground, sat his gift for his father, this time it was its normal size. Jack started making his way to it, but pillars of fire shot up to block him wherever he tried walk.

"Uh uh, that's against the rules," the host said as the fire danced in his eyes and anger coated his voice. They quickly changed back to his cheerful tone and blue eyes a moment later as the flames died down. "Now, let's move on to the second round. Question number two—what's in the second cage?"

Jack hurried, determined not to run out of time, and said the first thing that came to his mind. He could feel the sweat bead on his forehead. He was unsure if the heat of the extinguished flames or nervousness had caused the sweat, but he tried to concentrate. *If the gift to my dad was in cage one, then cage two might have . . .* "Mom?"

"That is correct! Show him cage number two!" bellowed the host as applause came again and the second cage lit up, uncovering Jack's mom standing there. Her head drooped forward, but she was otherwise very still, as if she had simply fallen asleep standing up.

"Mom!" Jack screamed. "Mom, wake up!"

"Alright, Jack, you've gotten one wrong answer and one right answer. One more right and you've won your right to choose. However, one more wrong and you lose it all, and she will never wake up," Ted explained. "That dream sand can be very strong," the host said to the audience as he laughed and the audience followed along. "So, Jackie Boy, are you ready to play?"

It was a lot to conceive, and Jack doubted he could actually save them both. There were no cages left for him to be questioned with, and he couldn't help but continue yelling for his mother in a defeated voice. "Mom, please wake up!"

"Alright, then let's get to it!" replied the host, ignoring Jack. "For your last and final question. How did you spot the streaking piece of metal that caused your flat tire?"

Jack was taken aback. This wasn't at all a question he had expected. He had thought, whatever the question was, it would have something to do with Sonny being the answer. He had no ideas of how he had spotted it the first day, but as he stared at his mother's head, tilted forward in slumber, he heard it. Something whispered to him. It repeated over and over again as the host began to speak again, but Jack couldn't make out what it was saying or where it was coming from.

"Three seconds until the buzzer," the host announced as Jack strained to hear the voice.

It sounded like, "Two parks, two trees."

"Two seconds," the host warned. Jack could just barely make sense of the whisper. "One," said the host with that dazzling white smile and fire in his eyes.

*Two dark, two keys?* Jack wondered frantically.

"Time's up, Jack!" the host shouted, just as Jack realized the voice was saying, "It's too dark too see."

"The flashlight!" Jack yelled, waking up from his dream. He was back in his own bed. His mother walked into his room just as she had the day before and the day before that, wearing the same pinstriped pants and red sweater.

"Jack, are you up yet?" asked his mother. "It's time to get ready to leave. Did you sleep alright?"

Jack awoke, holding his flashlight in his hand as if he'd been holding it the entire time, staring through the magnifying-glass handle up at the ceiling fan. "Yeah, Mom," he stated, just as before. "I'm awake." Then he got out of bed and made his way to the bathroom to get ready for their trip.

This day continued on just as the others had. Jack's mom was making breakfast, and he walked in as she stashed the tear-stained photo. After eating, they met outside, where Mrs. Johnson had her brief conversation before they were off once more. The drive seemed even longer with Jack's anticipation of hopefully ending this nightmarish loop. And, this time, he didn't forget to ask about the bathroom. His mother keyed restroom into the GPS unit, and they were instantly guided to their intended destination and the flat tire.

Jack pulled out his magnifying glass, now believing he hadn't seen the falling piece of metal because it was so far away. The reflecting light would be easier to see through the eyepiece. So he watched through the clear glass, looking up at the sky as they passed by trees and other buildings, until he was sure the timing was right and that his eyes were scanning the area.

He could almost count the seconds to when the tire would blow. Just a few more and he would know. They drove, getting closer to the rest area and old buildings. Then finally, after what seemed like the longest car ride he'd been on yet, gleaming high above them and streaking down quickly was a sparkling piece of metal falling through the air like a shooting star. It landed on the ground as if it had been thrown at them.

Jack watched, surprised and confused about where it had come from, as it came down. It didn't make sense, but he decided to wait for Sonny before thinking too hard about it. Then, just as he knew it would, the tire blew with a loud pop. Jack stared at the old building as his mom got out of the car to check the tire. There was definitely something going on with this area that he couldn't understand.

He went to the rest area, used the bathroom, and then waited for the wind to calm before going behind the rest area to wait for Sonny. After a few minutes of waiting, he saw her walk around the corner. She looked almost apprehensive, as if she were staring at a big dog. She seemed afraid to approach him at first.

"What are my plans for the future?" she asked Jack with a serious expression.

Glaring at her and caught completely off guard, Jack wondered if this was some kind of riddle. "What? Why?" he asked. She began to look threatened and backed away until he hastily answered, "A reporter or a journalist, I think."

"Okay. I had to make sure it was actually you, Jack. I still haven't ruled out any possibilities of what's going on. So, as far as I know, you could be an alien. This could be a huge cover-up and we were possibly overlooked," Sonny explained.

Jack hadn't thought much about that. She had appeared intelligent enough the last few days, but now she seemed paranoid. Of course, it was possible this could be bigger than he imagined. It was possible that aliens or the government—or something worse—was involved. Sonny's eyes never left his as she waited.

"So what did you find out?" she asked hurriedly.

"Well, it's a bit confusing, but I have a theory," Jack assured her. "The piece of metal fell from a lot higher than I realized before, so it could have come from either one of two things. Either some kind of flying object, like your alien theory." His face implied that he was highly skeptical of this theory. "Or it could have been from a tall building."

"Well, it can't be anything flying, or we would have seen it . . . unless it's invisible," Sonny said, waving off that idea. "Or maybe if it was higher than we can view?"

Jack had seen enough science fiction to know that wasn't possible. "The metal would've burned up before it landed, or at the very least made a bigger dent in the road," Jack said in a matter-of-fact tone.

Sonny looked around the corner. "Maybe someone threw it from one of the buildings across the street?"

"I thought of that too, but none of the buildings near here are tall enough to throw it from the direction it came from," Jack stated. "It's hard to explain, but I know there's something strange about that really beat-up one across from here. But there's not even a second floor on it, so how could it come from so high?" Jack asked.

Studying the ground, she took out her notepad and began clicking her pen frantically. Once she appeared to have come to a conclusion, she asked him, "Where do you go when you leave here? Do you go straight to Maryland?"

"No, my mom can't get a tire 'til tomorrow. So we get a room at a hotel a few blocks from here. Why? What's up?" Jack asked hopefully.

"I think I have a plan. From what you've discovered so far, seems as if we need to check out that building," Sonny said, looking over her shoulder. "We don't have time to do it now. My father's been preoccupied lately, so it shouldn't be a problem for me. But do you think you can sneak out and meet me here tonight when your mother falls asleep?"

Jack blinked a few times. He knew he wasn't exactly a stranger to getting into trouble at school, but sneaking out in an unfamiliar town was a new level. "I don't even know if I could get away with it," Jack said, feeling a bit cowardly.

"I understand how you must feel, but I can't do this alone. Not when I've found someone who knows what I know. We may be able to do something about it," she said, becoming more and more persuasive. "Besides, even if you do get caught, your mother won't remember it tomorrow if there is no tomorrow." She waited for him to answer. Jack thought about it, and even though he hated to admit it, he knew she was right. Finally, he succumbed to her persuasion.

"Okay. When do you want to meet?"

They considered it would be problematic if Jack would somehow instantly be back in his bed at home or vanish altogether if they waited until after midnight, so they decided to meet before the day could cross over. That night, after his mother was fully asleep, Jack snuck out of their hotel room. It was almost a quarter to eleven as he walked through the hotel's doors. Luckily, no one seemed to notice him since there was no one attending the front desk to stop him.

Going through the glass doors, he could feel how much colder it was now that it was night. As the wind blew, he clung to his jacket, feeling the flashlight in his pocket against his side. He walked for several minutes before seeing the rest area where Sonny was waiting for him. Jack ran over to her, taking notice that she was still wearing short sleeves in the freezing night air.

"Aren't you cold?" Jack asked as he approached. "You wore a coat the first day I met you, but now it's like you don't even feel it."

Sonny looked down at her arms as if only now detecting that it was a little strange. "I don't know. I haven't felt cold since the day we met. . . . Maybe it's all connected or it's excitement? Well, we only have a few minutes before midnight, so we better hurry. What's that?" Sunny asked, pointing to Jack's hand.

He had brought out his flashlight from the inner pocket of his jacket almost unconsciously. "Oh, it's this detective's flashlight that my dad left me last Christmas. I figured we might need it when we go inside," Jack stated, discreetly placing it back into his pocket. "Might be dark in there."

"A flashlight?" she said, realizing he'd thought of something that should have been obvious to her. "Why didn't I think of that? Oh well, come on. There're no cars coming."

They made their way across the street to the broken-down building. The gargoyle statues seemed to breathe a waft of cold air when Jack and Sonny rushed by. Attempting to search the entire front, they realized early that everything was boarded up, except the front doors at the top of the stairs. As they climbed, Jack noticed the gold, shining sign on the right pillar. Now being close enough, he read it clearly.

"This building was built by JET Enterprises," he read aloud.

To get a better look at the date, Jack began rubbing the dirt off. He stopped when Sonny called him over.

"Jack, come here quickly," she whispered. "Do you hear that?"

Jack got closer to where she was standing near the front doors as it seemed to creak open just slightly more. "Yeah, I hear it," he whispered back. "It sounds like people shouting, but I don't see anyone inside."

The inside still seemed dark from the outside as they looked through the stained glass windows of the doors. But there was light coming from the opening. Crouching down, they tried to peek inside, but the small opening just wasn't wide enough. The wind began to pick up, as if to push them inside. Sonny glanced up to the top of the building, then back at Jack, and asked him, "Do you trust me?"

His heart beating quickly, he thought about the choices he had left: repeating days that may never end or venturing into an old and broken building that strongly resembled a haunted house he had dreamed of before. Glancing back in the direction of his hotel, he imagined his mother lying in bed, waiting for the next morning so they may reiterate the same daily conversation possibly forever. Staring back into Sonny's green eyes, her pupils now like orbs in the moonlight, he made a decision.

"I guess now's the best time to find out," he said honestly.

Taking his hand, Sonny smiled and whispered to him, "Let's go."

Then, dragging Jack behind her, she pulled the door open. They rushed into the once-dark building and were swallowed by a blinding light. The stunning light hit them as they entered the building, as if every area had spotlights on them. Jack began rubbing his eyes uncontrollably to adjust to it. Sonny attempted to raise her hand for shade as her eyes sparkled at the gold etchings and her mouth dropped at what she was witnessing. Jack could tell it had been quite some time since she was speechless, and he was only able to focus on her.

An elderly man with long white hair, elegant crimson-red pajamas, and matching bedroom slippers stopped abruptly in front of Jack, staring at him thoroughly through his spectacles. His thin gold chain swung slightly as he wavered in place.

"Can you tell me how to get home from here?" the man asked feebly.

Jack's eyes had finally adjusted but were still darting around the room, from person to person, as dozens of people bustled around in every direction like the tourists he'd seen during the last few days.

"I wish I knew what here was," he answered.

# Chapter 3
## A Fortunate Reading

From outside, they never would have guessed what was hidden inside the dark windows of the dilapidated building. However, once inside, they couldn't believe the outside could somehow be attached to something so incredible. Overwhelmed, they stood in a room more glamorous than anything they had ever imagined. Tall ceilings glittered with gold designs mirroring the stars outside and appeared to move with earth's rotation. Crystal chandeliers that hung high above, attached to nothing, overlooked the people running by. Following the black-etched white marble floors to each side were long hallways that appeared to go on indefinitely.

Placed in the center of the floor a short distance away was a large gray stone fountain with two large letter *H*'s engraved on it. At first glance, the fountain appeared to be like any other fountain with water jets shooting up. But as Sonny and Jack grew closer, they noticed several more holes like tiny dots on a basketball surrounding the larger holes. Water shot out in bright colors like fireworks, arranging the spray and mist together as if performing a ballet of colors. As the water landed in the fountain, chimes played in musical rhythm like a lullaby.

As they stared absently at the lobby, a few people in tourist clothes wandered around aimlessly. Dozens of bellhops dressed in red suits with gold buttons and lace rushed by in all directions. A few ran by with luggage covering their whole bodies so that the pieces of luggage appeared to be walking by themselves. Others came from the north with what looked like yellow caution tape clinging to their coats and shoes.

They were being ordered by a stern, older-looking man with dark skin and brown eyes. He wore a neatly pressed black suit. Jack could tell he was a no-nonsense type by the way he kept order but still appeared friendly enough. As they watched the bustle of people clamor around the doorway, they went completely unnoticed until Sonny interrupted the commotion.

"Excuse us," Sonny said timidly. "We . . . ,"

"Where's the doorman who was watching that entrance?!" yelled the man in the black suit, "No one is to enter or exit the building until the investigation is completed!"

A young bellhop with freckles came rushing up to his left side. "I'm sorry, sir, I was sure I sealed it before. It won't happen again," he said, placing a hand on the crease between the doors. A bright white glow surrounded them, and, in an instant, the doors had vanished completely, leaving a blank space on a solid wall, as if the doors had never existed.

"Wait," Jack said to the bellhop as their entrance, and therefore exit, disappeared. "What happened to the doors? We need to be able to get back out!"

"That'll be all, Number Fifty-Two. You should finish your training videos in the theater room now," said the overseer in black to the bellhop. From his tone, Jack thought it smart not to cross him.

"Yes, Number One," responded Fifty-Two. He walked away, past the fountain and out of view. The man in the black suit came over to Jack and Sonny and stared at them carefully, as if assessing them.

"I do apologize. He's still quite new. But until these matters are settled, neither guests nor employees are permitted to enter or exit the premises," the man in the black suit stated flatly. "Hmm. You both seem different, even for dreamers."

"What do you mean? Where exactly are we?" Sonny asked, displaced.

"Oh, forgive my rudeness," said the man as he straightened his tie. "I am Number One, the manager and keeper of information of this establishment. You have the honor of finding yourself in a grand establishment. The Holiday Hotel."

"Number One?" Sonny asked. "That's a peculiar name."

"No, my dear, that is my position here at the hotel," the manager said with dignity. "All of my floor associates go by number, because there are so many. The doorman, Number Fifty-Two, who was just here, is actually Thomas and my name is Emanuel. Each attendant is given a number that corresponds to the floor they attend to. At this establishment, the first floor is the top of the building, leading here to the fifty-second floor. Normally, I attend to the top floor, but I like to stay close to the newer employees. I visit the ground floor often because of this."

"Wait. This is a hotel?" Jack asked in confusion.

"Yes, for vacationing spirits," Emanuel explained.

Jack glanced around the hall and chuckled. "Really? You mean ghosts?" he asked skeptically.

Number One was taken aback. "Please refrain from using the 'G word' here. That is an offensive and derogatory term for us. We prefer the term 'spirits' or 'the living impaired.' We have many holiday spirits who are currently staying with us. I suppose you would consider them the celebrities of our existence."

Sonny grinned from ear to ear. "Do you mean like Santa Clause? Is he staying here?" Jack wasn't sure if she was being sarcastic or not, but at second glance, he could tell she was genuinely hopeful.

"Of course not," stated the manager, who, to Sonny's disappointment, was almost amused by the idea. "This is his busiest time of the year. What would he be doing vacationing now? Besides, Santa is not a holiday spirit. He is a symbol who works with the Spirit of Christmas."

"You can't really expect us to believe all of this," Jack stated simply. "Santa Clause isn't real. I'm probably just having another dream that I'll wake up from soon. He's just a myth from a story."

"And where do you believe the stories come from, young man?" the manager asked defiantly. "I suppose you believe every story you've read was created randomly from nowhere? You would be quite surprised how many of these 'myths' have true bases."

"Okay. Well, why does the building look abandoned on the outside?" Jack asked, trying his best to keep up.

"That would be the haze," Emanuel pointed out as the confused expression on Jack's face heightened. "It may be more difficult to explain that. The haze distracts people like you from seeing places and buildings like these. It separates our world from yours, but in the same space."

Instinctively, Sonny brought out her notepad and pen. "Like another plane of existence?"

"That is one way to describe it." Emanuel continued his explanation. "Both exist simultaneously together but on different planes of existence, as you said. They only exist subconsciously to each other, which allows you to view your own existence normally. But, somehow, you are able to see ours as well."

Though he had only known Sonny for a few days, Jack had never seen her as speechless as she was now. He realized she must be thinking of the same question he was. "So, if we're not supposed to see this plane of existence, how is that we're here?" Jack asked cautiously. "Are we dead?"

"No, you are both currently alive," the manager said flatly, "It is true, we rarely get dreamers here, but it does happen occasionally. However, there is something particularly special about you both."

Jack wasn't thrilled about how he had said "currently alive." Yet, excitement filled Sonny as she regained her voice. "Do all spirits come here? Maybe my Granddad is here?"

"My apologies, but this is a hotel for holiday spirits and symbols. Besides the attendants who work here and a few holiday symbols, no other guests stay here," Emanuel stated sympathetically. "All of the attendants under my care I know personally, and they are chosen as one of the fifty-two for a number of reasons. One being they have no families, which allows them to be away for lengthy periods."

Obviously disappointed, Sonny continued to ask questions. "If we're not spirits, why is it we can see through this haze, but no one else can? Why are the days repeating, and what exactly are dreamers and holiday spirits?"

"Yeah?" Jack spoke. "Isn't it just a feeling?"

Just then, an attendant with a particularly large amount of yellow tape stuck to her shoe ran up to Emanuel. She was clearly out of breath. "Excuse me . . . Number One," she panted. She had a thick accent that Jack tried to distinguish between British or Australian, but as she was out of breath, it was difficult to tell.

"I'm with guests right now, Forty-Three. Is this something Number Two can handle?" he asked.

Number Forty-Three looked unsure whether she should continue, but she did anyway. "It's rather important, sir. We've discovered what went missing."

After blinking a few times, Emanuel excused himself and spoke to Number Forty-Three privately. When he returned, he appeared to be in a hurry. "I do apologize, but I must send for assistance," he said anxiously, walking them to the manager's desk.

Bringing out a guest list, Emanuel asked Sonny and Jack to sign in and handed them each a packet from the desk. "Now, here are your maps and key cards. Since the doors have been sealed, I have compensated your stay here. You will travel past the fountain to the televators on your right. Choose the fourteenth floor, and your rooms are four and five. I believe you'll be quite comfortable with the temperature on that floor. Breakfast will be served in the dining hall when you wake. Now, I really must get some attendants to the first floor, so if you need anything at all, you may use the phone for room service. Please refrain from getting into any trouble. The last thing I need is two dreamers being added to my trainee list."

Once they were signed in, Emanuel handed the guest list to Number Forty-Three, who disappeared down the west hall. Jack and Sonny took the key cards, thanked Emanuel, and followed the path on the right side of the fountain. They tried their best to stay out of the way of all the attendants pushing carts as they made their way to the sign.

"I thought I heard him incorrectly, but it really does say 'televators,'" Sonny said to Jack. "Wonder what's so special about it?"

"I don't know, but I'm still wondering when we can leave," Jack said, thinking about his parents. "Wish someone would explain what's going on here and why the days are repeating."

The doors of the televator opened up to a cylindrical room with silver walls. Over fifty buttons, each with a blue light, lined the wall all around them and lit up the room in a blue glow. They had to look in every direction before finding the button to the fourteenth floor.

"Here it is," Jack said as he pressed the button. The doors closed and all the lit buttons went out except the one he had pressed. In an instant, they came back on and a bell rang, even though they hadn't seemed to move yet. "Wait, we can't be there already," Jack said, watching the doors open. "We haven't even moved."

The televator doors opened and revealed a new hall with seven doors lining its left side and a blank wall on the other. The hallway was decorated in spring colors. Pink, yellow, green, and blue flowers hung over the doors and waved in a warm breeze. The smell like the air just after a rainfall filled the hall. Sonny walked forward, reading the numbers on the first door. Jack followed behind her after studying the wall of buttons they were leaving. "I think it's a teleporter. That's how we got here so fast."

Sonny didn't seem to hear him as she was standing near the end of the hall, looking at the bare wall across from their rooms. As Jack walked closer, she put her finger to her lips, signaling him to be very quiet. He crept slowly toward her as she drew near the wall and pressed her ear against it.

"What is it?" Jack asked as quietly as possible.

"I don't know, but I could swear I heard laughing coming from behind here, then it stopped," she said, still looking at the blank wall.

It was quiet, and all was still for a few moments, until Jack turned around and went to door number five. Sonny brought out her pad and pen from her back pocket and began jotting down notes. When she was finished, she placed them back in her pocket and walked to door number four.

"Well, I guess we might as well get some sleep," Sonny said with a stifled yawn. "Hopefully, they'll figure out what's going on with the days, and we can leave tomorrow, so you can get to your father."

"Yeah, hopefully," Jack replied as a thought occurred to him. "You don't think we'll end back up at our houses again, do you?"

She pulled a key card from her packet and opened her door as she spoke. "If that were true, we would just end back up where we started. For all I know, we could be dreaming like you said. Maybe abducted by the government and drugged. Suppose we'll find out tomorrow, if there is a tomorrow. Either way, I'm sure we'll come up with a plan. It could be an impressive story."

Ideas of never getting to his father and leaving his mother alone unnerved him as he stood in front of his door. "I'm not really tired yet. I think I'm gonna have a look around downstairs before going to bed. Check out the lobby, maybe."

"Alright, don't go sneaking out without me," she said as she closed the door.

After taking the televator back to the ground floor, Jack found himself in an almost-empty lobby. A few attendants were still around, but since they were working, they didn't stay long. The fountain's water spurts had slowed down to match the stillness of night as dark blues crossed paths with purples. Behind the manager's desk, Emanuel was nowhere to be found. Jack assumed he was still taking care of whatever was discovered by Number Forty-Three.

*So, something has gone missing,* Jack thought to himself. He wondered if it had anything to do with how he and Sonny had gotten there, or possibly the reason for the repeating days.

From the packet he was given, he brought out the brochure that included the hotel map and locations of interest. Apparently, the hall was much larger than he had realized, because the brochure listed three hundred sixty-six places of interest on the ground floor, from the east to west hall. Only seven of which were guest rooms on this floor. They included everything from gift shops and coffee shops to an arcade dungeon, The Lucky Coin Casino, and a place called Cloud Surf N' Turf. Unsure of what he was looking for, Jack began walking and randomly placed his finger on the list of places before stopping at one called The Candy Garden. A yellow path appeared on the map, showing the exact distance and direction from where he stood to The Candy Garden.

Following the path, he walked down the long west hall for several minutes. It had been dressed in a peaceful wintery scene that became noticeably colder as he continued. The doors were colored in a pine green resembling forest trees, and the walls were snowy white. Every door had a sign above it with the name of the room inside. He passed by Diamond's Jewelry Shop, Frank's Famous Fruits, and Pets Imagined. As he continued walking, he came across a white door with red, slanted stripes like a candy cane. The sign above it read "Marilyn's Candy Garden: Sweets, Treats, and Other Eats." The knob held an additional, smaller sign that asked everyone not to eat the door. An alluring smell of peppermint came from it. Because it was so late at night (or early in the morning, depending on your preference), he knocked, unsure if they were closed. However, the door opened quickly, and he feared he may have awoken an employee. A thin, tall man wearing a short brown top hat, a pink shirt, and a white apron cracked the door, smiling slightly.

"Can I help you?" asked the man in the apron.

"I was hoping to see The Candy Garden, I guess?" Jack asked timidly.

The tall man's smile widened as much as the door as he opened it more. "Well, of course you are. Come in, come in," he said, welcoming Jack inside. "Marilyn is unavailable at the moment, but I'd be more than happy to assist you."

Jack followed the tall man inside. His shirt revealed that his name was Chip, as it was printed on the back of his shirt. Chip escorted Jack past empty, delicately placed white chairs and glass tables that were arranged as if the room were made to look like a tea shop. The back of the room held a blank white wall with pink writing spelling out the word *sweet*. In front of the wall, a register sat atop a counter with barstools for people to sit on. Jack looked in every direction, but he didn't see anything spectacular about this room. Reaching the counter, Jack waited in front of it as Chip punched a few keys on the register. The wall behind him shuddered and began to split open.

"This way, sir." Chip gestured toward the split wall.

Hesitantly, Jack walked inside the open area and found himself embraced by a lavish garden made entirely of candies, chocolates, cookies, cakes, and tarts. Various lively flowers made from licorice and gum drops appeared to bloom vigorously from a field of grass made of icing. Large fountains made of chocolate sprayed chocolate into a pond. Yet the most impressive piece was the castle in the center, made entirely of cake and tarts with white-chocolate frosting and pink icing. It was surrounded by a chocolate moat leading from the fountain, and a labyrinth wall made of sugar cookies and green-frosting grass surrounded the moat.

"Everything here is edible and has been compensated by the manager," said Chip, watching Jack's stunned expression. "Please do enjoy yourself," he said, leaving Jack inside with a huge smile on his face.

Jack knew he'd read a story about a place like this before. It reminded him of something Emanuel had mentioned to Jack about where the stories come from. After looking at the fountain, he shrugged it off and continued into the garden.

With a bag of treats in his hand and a t-shirt from The Candy Garden that said "Don't be a sucker, visit The Candy Garden," Jack tracked his next destination to the Arcade

Dungeon, where he experienced shooting virtual dragons with a laser gun and battling virtual knights with a saber while mounted on a black steed.

It seemed as if hours had passed while he'd gone from place to place, discovering what the hotel had to offer. The Adrenaline Room allowed him to simulate skydiving, and the Fantasy Track gave him the ability to ride on any vehicle he could imagine as he flew around on a hover board. He peeked into a room that seemed to be a valley where snow was falling and another that was swelteringly hot, like a desert.

Once it had gotten very late, his body began to drag on, and he became extremely tired. He decided to make his last trip to Bountiful Beverages to get a drink and then head to his room. On his way out of the Fantasy Track to the last shop, he overheard two attendants talking. As he left the room, he witnessed Number Forty-Three, with the piece of yellow tape still on her shoe, and the doorman, Number Fifty-Two, walking past without noticing him.

"I don't understand how it's possible after all these years," said Number Forty-Three. "That's a very powerful spirit. It's not like he could come to a sticky end so easily. You don't think he just ran away with it, do you, Thomas?"

"Of course not," Thomas replied. "Personally, I think he's been taken and the hourglass along with him. I just don't understand how. Who would be strong enough to overpower a holiday spirit here?"

Keeping his distance behind them, Jack crept along, eavesdropping and ducking into archways in the hall whenever they seemed about to turn around. He knew it was wrong to be listening in on their conversation, but he couldn't help but be interested. The only thing on his mind was that he had to do whatever it took to make it back to his parents.

"I'm still not sure how those two dreamers got in. I'm positive I sealed those doors once before," Number Fifty-Two stated flatly. "Number One said it's been close to twenty years or so since a dreamer has shown up."

"You think they had something to do with it?" Number Forty-Three asked. "I mean, if they worked themselves in here, might be a reason."

"Be serious, Millie, you know the owner and Number One are the only ones with access through locked doors here," Thomas said, pointing out the obvious. "I doubt they even know what's been going on. The boy did look slightly familiar, though. I was informed to consider them as possible suspects."

"So was I. I know it was before your time, but seems to be happening just like before with that so-called doctor and Father aiding him," she said as Number Fifty-Two stopped her abruptly.

"Shhh," he said quietly. "Be careful with the accusations. You know what Number One said about keeping this quiet from the guests, bringing up past events."

Number Forty-Three waved as if the thought amused her. "Oh, come off it. No one's that oblivious. You know, just as I do, that everyone knows what's going on. Once again, it all points to him, doesn't it? I'm just glad I'm on the floor above his, or I might be as shaky as Number Forty-Four has been. Not to mention Number Seven has been fairly steamed since the doctor arrived on his floor."

"True, he doesn't seem the same," agreed Number Fifty-Two. "Wasn't he the last holiday to see the owner?"

"Yup. Been locked up in his room since this mess started," she said. "Been strange no one's seen him recently. And Number One has been takin' the mick' right outta us since, hasn't he?"

They paused for a moment, and Jack was sure they had noticed him. But Thomas had only stopped to remove the piece of yellow tape from Millie's shoe. "I really don't blame Number One, with everything he's got to worry about now," Thomas continued. "Things go missing and he's held responsible. No wonder he's on edge."

A few rooms farther and they would be back at the entrance of the lobby. Jack tried his hardest to continue listening and keep his distance as Number Forty-Three got quiet. "Did you notice it all started the same day that woman got here."

"Yeah, she was creeping out some of the other attendants when she came in," stated Number Fifty-Two as they rounded the corner. "It was like she knew exactly what we were going to ask her. Then, she says she was sent here to wait, and I haven't heard from her since."

Watching them walk out of earshot, Jack decided to continue on to the east hall to Bountiful Beverages for his drink as he tried to figure out what it was all about. A spirit had gone missing, and a mysterious woman had showed up. None of it made sense, and he considered waking Sonny to keep notes. She seemed more familiar with strange things than he was. However, it was late; so he thought it better to wait and decided it was something that could hold off until morning.

As he walked the long hall and came closer to his destination, holiday decorations became more apparent. The farther he went, the colder the air became until he reached a sign that read Bountiful Beverages. After knocking a few times with no answer, he reached for a door handle before he noticed it didn't exist. There was no knob, sensor, scanners, or even a slot for a room key. Looking back at the other doors, he noticed they all had slots for cards and handles, but not this one—as if this hotel weren't odd enough. Jack was ready to head back to his room when the door opened mysteriously.

"Little earlier than I expected, but I've been waiting for you, Mr. Taylor," said a woman's voice in a thick European accent. Carefully, Jack entered the room, and the door slammed closed after him. He turned around quickly, feeling for a handle or something to open the door. However, there was nothing to pull on this side, either.

Jack began by saying, "How did you—" But the woman cut in as if knowing what he was thinking.

"Open and close the door?" she said, shuffling a deck of cards without looking up. "The rooms here are specifically tailored to each of us. So, in my room, the door opens automatically only for those whose presence I wish to be in."

It wasn't until then that Jack noticed the surroundings he had been admitted into. Instead of a room, he stood inside a large tent with gold tassels. It seemed to have more rooms on either side. Colorful pillows in purple, blue, and orange covered much of the floor. The edges of the room were harder to see, because it was poorly lit. Only the candles around the woman and a glowing sphere on a small silk-cloth-covered table in front of her lit the area. She motioned for Jack to sit as she shuffled a few cards. He stood there, straining to see her face as her hair and the shadows hid it from sight.

"I think I may have the wrong room," Jack said, backing up against the door. "I was just looking for a soda."

"I have your drink here," said the woman as she pointed to a glass mug filled with an orange liquid with a foamy top. "Now, please sit. Time is one thing we don't have much of."

Jack slowly sat down on one of the pillows and looked suspiciously at the frothy orange drink. "Who are you exactly?" he asked.

After placing five cards facedown on the table, she looked up, and Jack could finally see her face. The woman was enchantingly beautiful. She wore a red silk scarf that covered the top of her long, dark brown curly hair as it framed her tan face. The dress she wore had as many colors as the pillows but in shades of blue, red, and tan. It started at her shoulders and reached to her boots. A brown satin sash encircled her waist and gently followed her body's delicate curves.

"I am Luminista," said the woman. "But I don't think it is who I am that interests you as much as what I do." She stared at him with her hazel eyes as if looking directly into his heart. "I am the Romani fortune teller you've heard about recently."

For a moment, Jack wasn't sure she was serious. "You mean a Gypsy?" he asked, wondering how she knew he had been eavesdropping.

"Titles get confusing for people," Luminista said, waving off his question. "It is not important. What is important is that I was asked to wait for you in this hotel to give you a reading."

"Someone knew I would come here?" Jack asked in astonishment. "Who?"

"Myself, of course," the woman said indignantly. "Do not think I don't sense the skepticism in your voice. I urge you to believe this is very much real, and you do not have time to be skeptical. Now, I do not claim to tell futures like the psychics you've heard of who claim to. Only oracles can do that. I read future paths depending on the decisions you make. As your choices change, paths change. It is my job to know more about the art of reading the cards than anyone. However, as everything I tell you changes one possibility to another, I can only give you broad readings."

She took a deep breath and closed her eyes as if attempting to remember something from some time ago. "What I can tell you is that I did a reading for a man in the city. With what that man learned from me, he paid me to come here when the time was right to do a reading for a boy. The description that was given to him was a boy with the duties of a tailor, who travels with the moon in his pocket, and who befriends the sun, looking to quench his thirst."

Instinctively, Jack checked his pocket for his flashlight. "Befriends the sun?" he asked himself. "You mean Sonny?"

"I simply translate the cards to the best of my abilities," Luminista replied, smiling slightly. "I was not sure when your exact arrival would be. However, I sensed it to be during the coldest months. So I came here on the twenty-first, the first day of winter, and I have been waiting for days to have you choose your card."

"But I'm not a tailor," Jack said. Then he realized what she meant. "Wait, you mean Taylor? Is that how you knew my last name?"

Watching closely, the fortune teller smiled and gestured for Jack to choose from one of the five cards on the table. His hand hovered over the first few cards before he finally picked up the fifth. Before he was able to look at it, she quickly snatched it, placed it into a tan envelope, and handed it to him.

"You will open this, revealing your card as well as the answer to a question you have not asked but will when the time is right," said the fortune teller, shuffling the cards back into the deck. The glowing sphere between them grew brighter as she laid down a card from the top of the deck. "This is the fool card. He is the spark that sets everything into motion. The cause of all effects, no matter how small, can be the seeds of an unknown end. This is where your new journey will begin. Be careful with the fool, as he is tricky. How you interact with him can either aid you or make a fool of you as well."

Taking the next card from the deck, she laid it down next to the fool. "Hmm. The magician card. Now this is the creator of that which the fool starts. His manipulation of basic elements is so divine to the physical world, his magic seems to be unparalleled. Be warned; do not let his tricks shadow your mind before attempting to brighten his with tricks of your own."

She placed a third card down by the other two as Jack dearly wished he had woken Sonny so she could be writing all this down. "The justice card. The cards are not bound by the physical world and, for that, neither is justice. This card's meanings are dual in that those doing good deeds will be rewarded, while those who violate natural laws will be punished. The path you choose will challenge your strengths and weaknesses, and justice will decide what you deserve when all is done. Now, for the final card. . . ."

Watching closely, Jack became very still when he saw the picture on the final card. The eternal, empty eyes stared back at him from a spectral horse charging the field. "The death card," Luminista said quietly, watching Jack's eyes. "Hmm. Interesting response."

Checking all around him and wondering what she was looking at, Jack asked, "What's interesting?"

"Your expression is different from most who witness the death card. Those who view this card flush with fear, but in you . . . in you, I almost sense hatred. As if being reunited with an old enemy you've battled before. . . ."

His eyes never left the card as she explained its meaning. "You see, those who fear the death card are fools themselves, of course. Images of Death galloping through a field bring fear to the eyes of many, because it is the greatest unknown. It is truly one of the most powerful cards in the art, as well as the most misunderstood."

Jack scratched his head. "Misunderstood? It doesn't mean I'll die?"

Shaking her head, she laughed. "We all must die someday, but that does not mean that is what the card predicts. Everyone fears the unknown, and since death is the ultimate unknown, it is naturally man's greatest fear. This card's purest meaning, however, is only of transformation. Shedding old beliefs and gaining intellect are both transformations that you should embrace. Some see the death card and immediately think of a grim future. The death card more commonly illustrates the death of one's past self into one's new self."

His eyes darted to the orange drink, wondering if it really was safe or if this reading was leading him to be poisoned. His throat had become dry like chalk, and he was ready to give in.

"It is safe to drink, I promise you," she said reassuringly.

Bringing the orange drink to his lips, Jack could smell mint, orange, vanilla ice cream, mango, and banana all at once, as if it were sprinting up his nose. As he sipped, an explosion of flavors engulfed his tongue and he smiled. "This is incredible. I feel like I could run twenty marathons. What is it?"

"It's a drink called Fiz, made originally in the city," the fortune teller said as she gathered the cards. "That's the island cream flavor. I chose that flavor specifically for you, because I sensed you liked citrus, though its energetic effects won't last long." Her voice trailed off as she picked up the death card.

Jack placed the empty glass down, feeling both the last bits of the cold drink in his mouth and the warm energy it gave him as he wiped the foam off his upper lip. "What's wrong?" he asked, watching dread fill her face.

"This shouldn't be," said Luminista in an eerie voice. "There is another card stuck beneath the death card."

"Like a mistake?" asked Jack, bouncing with energy from the drink. "Which one is mine?"

"The art does not make mistakes," Luminista explained, flipping over the additional card. "They are all yours. It hints at what can and what will. These cards being attached would mean they travel together."

"I'm not so sure I want to know what it means," he stated sullenly.

"This is the world card," she stated as the glowing ball grew brighter. "This card shows us the new beginning from whatever is left. The fool's journey ends. The magician's tricks are done. Justice has willed out, and the cycle is complete for the transformation. The new beginning is all that is left, but the beginning of what is the mystery. This card being attached to the death card tells us that a transformation will change the entire world. It is odd that you did not fear the death card, but with this one, I feel it will weigh on you heavily. I believe you've already guessed what this means. Even I would never have foretold how important you were, until now."

"How important I am?" he asked, taken aback. "Why me?"

"Because, Mr. Taylor," Luminista replied as the ball filled with smoke and the candles brightened slightly, then went out completely. "These five cards depict five parts of a journey you will undertake. With that, decisions you make will either renew the world or destroy it as we know it now."

Silence filled the room as the candles re-lit themselves. Scanning the room, Jack looked in every direction, but the fortune teller had vanished. The door behind him opened slowly. Carefully, he stood up and exited the room, leaving it empty except for the few pillows and the ball that lay atop the table. The door closed quietly behind him, sealing itself again.

Carrying the tan envelope Luminista had given him, he followed the path of the hall. The effects of the Island Cream Fiz were wearing off, and Jack began feeling drowsy again. The pasty white walls and green doors began to blur into colorful spots. Once at the main lobby, he noticed Number Fifty-Two standing back by the wall where the doors had once been as if he were awaiting orders. He nodded his head at Jack and continued to wait. The manager was back at his desk, and as Jack walked by, he raised an eyebrow, as if wondering what Jack was still doing up. Making his way to the televator, past the almost-still waters flowing from the fountain, he wondered if spirits had bathrooms, because he really had to use one now.

Once on the fourteenth floor, he shuffled with the envelope and map packet before bringing out his key card and placing it in his room's key slot. Stepping inside the room was like stepping inside the hotel all over again, except it was tailored perfectly for him. The walls were in his favorite shade of blue. Instead of a poster, an entire mural of his favorite football player was painted behind an enormous plush bed. Across from the bed stood a large flat screen TV with gaming systems and detective movies ready. On the nightstand was a stack of detective books, including *The Big Guide to Finding Clues* and others he'd never read before. Placed atop another nightstand was a box for his flashlight. Beside that nightstand was a small fridge. Next to a door leading to the restroom was a large window at the end of the room. It overlooked the city below.

After using the restroom, he placed the flashlight into the box. The inside was lined with a soft dark-blue material and the outside was decorated in silver with the hotel's engraving. When he opened the refrigerator underneath, he found several bottles of Fiz drinks. Some were yellow, red, or green. Even the island cream flavor in orange was there.

It was then that Jack remembered the additional card in the envelope he had received from Luminista. As he began to open it, he sat on the bed and immediately felt his eyes become heavier as a wave of uncontrolled yawning flooded out. Naturally, he laid his head on the pillow before removing the contents from the tan packaging. Before he had a glimpse of anything inside, he instantly fell asleep as if a switch had been turned off. A note along with the card slid out of the envelope and dropped to the floor. The card depicted an image of a bright star hovering over a sleeping boy on a field

# Chapter 4
## *Fatherly Advice*

Awaking the next morning, Jack felt completely rested for a change. The sun came peeking into the room, bringing in a dull light, as if nothing about the day were unusual. Not only was he not feeling the effects of the repeating day, but he also couldn't even remember dreaming. He'd had no nightmares or shock waking up, and, more importantly, he was still in the same place that he'd fallen asleep. He wasn't sure if he was relieved by this or more panicked that it had all been real. Mostly, he was concerned that he couldn't remember falling asleep. Because the morning was so peaceful, he didn't allow it to bother him much before getting up.

Leaping out of bed, he ran directly to the window, where the sun greeted him warmly. He hadn't realized how high up he was. Birds flew by, apparently unaware that the building he stood in was even there. Tiny cars resembling scurrying ants raced by the rest area and tire shop. Silently, he hoped his mother wouldn't worry too much about him being gone. He wondered if she would even know or if there was a cloned version of him down there somewhere. Mostly, he just wanted to know when the doors of the hotel would open so he could be with his father again.

After showering, he looked inside the closet, forgetting that everything he had packed would still be at home now. To his delight, however, clothes that were perfectly tailored to his size appeared in the closet, hung ready to be worn. There were not only a few of his own clothes, including his favorite pair of jeans, but also new, expensive clothes he'd never dreamed of owning. He put on a pair of black jeans that had extra pockets for his flashlight. Then he chose a new shirt in his second-favorite color of blue that read "get a clue" in white letters. He pulled on a new black bomber-style leather jacket that matched his hair color and a pair of white skater sneakers.

After getting ready, he stepped outside of his room. On his way to get breakfast, he stopped to knock on Sonny's door. She seemed to be thinking the same as he was, because she stepped out of her room at that moment, as well.

"Looks like you found your way through the closet, too?" Sonny asked, smiling.

"Yeah, was there nothing new in yours?" Jack asked. Looking at her attire, he couldn't tell. It was almost the same thing she had worn before, but in different colors—a regular purple shirt with black jeans covered in her usual ink stains and sneakers. However, she wore a black-and-white knit hat today.

"I decided to wear some of my own things, instead. Quite comfortable in my own, you see. I was surprised they had a holder for my pen," she stated, holding her pen up. Jack hadn't taken much notice of it up close. It was uniquely red with a silver spiral clip going from the top all the way around it to the tip. "My grandfather left it to me. As long as I've had it, it has never run out of ink. Of course, that was the least surprising thing about it."

Just then, the sound of scuffling shoes came from the wall opposite their rooms. The sound of a telephone being hung up was followed by a door being opened and shut before a strange-looking man walked through the wall.

"Oh, wowzer!" he said with a wide, shocked expression. "Oh, that was a good scare. Very good, indeed. I must remember to write this down and try it soon. Where is my pen?" He patted his pockets. "Oh, may I borrow that?" He took the pen from Sonny and began writing in the air. Then he clicked the top. "Remember to write this down," he stated into it as he clicked it again.

"Remember to write this down," the pen repeated.

The man then handed it back to Sonny. "Thank you, my dear."

"Wait," Sonny said, truly confused. "This pen doesn't record," she said, clicking it a few times as it spouted ink all over her.

"Ha, ha, ha, ha!" cackled the strange man. "April Fool's! That was a good one, too!"

Jack couldn't believe this guy, and he was irritated. "Hey what's the matter with you?" he spoke up.

"Oh, don't worry. It's vanishing ink," the strange man said, motioning to Sonny's shirt and face as it, indeed, began dissolving. "See, all gone."

~ 75 ~

Sonny and Jack looked at each other and then at the odd man who was still smiling widely. He resembled a clown missing his makeup. He wore a white suit covered in yellow, green, and orange polka dots and a very large pink bow. His blond hair stood perfectly spiked as he grinned at them.

"I do love a good prank. So tell me, what *is* your favorite letter?" he asked.

"Favorite letter?" Jack asked.

"Yes, of the alphabet," responded the clown-like man, "My favorite letter is the *U*. So many wonderful words begin with *U*. Unique, united, ultimate, ultra, unoriginal, unorthodox, unparalleled, unbounded." He smiled. "Of course, as the Spirit of April Fool's Day, it's in my nature to enjoy good pranks in an unorthodox and unbounded matter . . . unnaturally." He chuckled.

"Really? You're the Spirit of April Fool's Day?" Jack asked skeptically as he tried his hardest to remember what the fortune teller had said about a fool. "Like a holiday spirit?"

"Yes, I am the great and powerful Fool. The one and only. Not to be duplicated, copied, or cloned. Undisputed king of all that is joking," the spirit said with glee as he walked toward the televator. "I must be off, however. I have someone I must meet, and I don't dare to dawdle and go missing too."

"What do you mean 'go missing'?" Sonny asked, "Who went missing?"

The Fool looked at her cautiously, and his smile faded slightly. "The holiday spirit who guards the hourglasses, of course. But trust me, it's not him you should be worried about. The so-called inventor is the one we should all avoid, but everyone knows that Mr. Shadow is the real shady one.

~ 76 ~

Trouble always follows that spirit, but I would be careful either way if I were you."

As he continued to the televator, he morphed his head into that of a shadowy, hooded figure. "Hope you're not afraid of what goes bump in the night," he said in an ominous voice that was followed by a chilling laugh, and then he was gone.

"Did you feel how cold it got?" Sonny said, rubbing her arms. She brought out her pad and checked her pen. After confirming it was normal, she began writing. "He must have one of those villas behind that wall. I wonder what it's like in there."

"How do you know he has a villa?" asked Jack as they walked to the televator.

"I did some research when I woke up this morning," she said, walking beside him. "I planned on doing it last night, but I fell asleep almost as soon as I lay down. Well, last night when I heard that noise behind the wall, I searched through the packet the manager gave us with the map. It shows locations for all the rooms, including these villas, but I couldn't understand it." She pulled out her pad from her back pocket again. It showed a hand-drawn replica of the hotel map. "It states there's a special room across from us, but there are no doors here."

Trying to take in everything Sonny was saying, Jack could only form one question. "When did you have time to redraw the entire map?" he asked, but she only laughed and told him it was a long story.

They took the televator down and made their way to the fifty-second floor. There were more guests roaming the lobby than the night before, and there was a long line coming from the dining hall. A few of the guests were complaining about being on a list and debating over colors. Just before it began to get rowdy, they noticed Emanuel, in his perfectly pressed black suit, at the front desk sending attendants to defuse the situation.

"Maybe he can tell us what's going on," Sonny said, optimistically walking to the front desk. "Hello, Manny," Sonny said, waving to the manager.

"My name is Emanuel, not Manny," the manager replied with dignity.

"So, Manny," Sonny proceeded, "What is all the commotion at the dining hall?"

Emanuel sighed. "Guests tend to always get rowdy around meal times. If you two are off to breakfast, I'd suggest you hurry and mind the new management's rules. He was only scheduled to have the room for one day, but as his good *luck* would have it, with the day repeating, he insists he is still under the guidelines of one day."

Sonny and Jack exchanged looks. "Do you think they may have something to do with what went missing or the repeating days?" Jack asked as the manager's eyes narrowed. "Seems like a motive to me, I mean."

"I assure you these matters are concerns you need not bother yourself with, and I would advise you not to continue. The staff and I will handle this just as quietly and swiftly as we can. As far as the holiday spirit you are accusing, I would dare say he is only looking to enjoy his vacation, not end all of existence." As Emanuel walked toward the televator, he turned to address Jack and Sonny. "Now, I just received an urgent call from the owner, and I am needed upstairs. Please keep yourselves out of trouble. Good day to you both."

They made their way to a line of guests who looked as if they were standing outside of a party. "What did he mean by 'end all of existence'?" Jack asked as they approached the dining room. "And is this really the dining hall?" Jack asked.

"I'm not sure, but I have my doubts he would tell us. . . . And it looks more like a nightclub," Sonny replied.

As they waited and made their way to the front of the line, they noticed a sign that read "dining room temporarily under the management of Lucky." Two large guards with a clipboard stood in front of a gold velvet rope blocking the door. They were identical, like twins, and muscular with matching red hair. The only difference between them was the full beard on the left one, who was wearing a green t-shirt that read "Blarney Stone Cor!" and the thick mustache on the right one, who was wearing a black t-shirt that read "Thirty-two Countries Strong."

After a few minutes of waiting in line, Jack and Sonny had made their way to the front and were stopped immediately. "Well, look what blew in, Michael," said the mustachioed guard with an Irish accent. "Looks like the lads be wanting to get inside the lounge."

"Aye, as if they could be deadly," replied the man called Michael, also with an Irish accent. He eyed Sonny over his folded arms. "Although the lass looks like she may have a bit of the Emerald Isle in her, Christopher. Reminds me of that Alice from Ms. Autumn's challenge."

"You know, I think you may be right, Michael. Not quite a skanger, though," Christopher agreed. "But what about the wanker she's with?"

"Hey, wanker," Michael said to Jack. "What's the craic?"

Jack wasn't sure what a *craic* was or what they were going on about, but he answered them the best he could. "We came to eat," replied Jack. "Can we get in?"

"You hear that, brother?" asked Michael sarcastically. "They wanna get into The Shamrock. You do realize this is not just any Irish pub, it's *the* Irish pub."

"Well, lounge, really," corrected Christopher.

"You always do that," complained Michael.

"Do what?" Christopher asked his brother.

"Correcting me in front of—" Michael began.

"Excuse me, gentlemen," Sonny cut in. "Can we please get into this lounge?"

"Well, that depends," said Michael.

"Yeah, that depends," repeated Christopher.

"You got the right color?" the brothers asked in unison.

Sonny looked back at Jack and shrugged, but he was already fumbling in his pockets for something. "Will this work?" Jack asked, holding his flashlight up to the guards. The guards smiled in apparent disappointment.

"Thought we'd have a little fun pinching the lad, too," said Christopher as he lifted the velvet rope blocking the doorway.

"Oh, well. Good man, yourself," said Michael, "Go on, you two."

Sonny led the way as Jack followed her into the lounge. "How'd you know?" she asked.

"Seemed obvious, with the Saint Patty theme," he replied. "Just lucky I had something green."

They walked into a room that was much bigger than they'd expected. Hundreds of guests were sitting in plush green lounge chairs at tables and listening to a band on stage. The chiming of slot machines spewing gold coins came from a smaller room to the side. A bartender behind a long glass bar table served bottles of Fiz. The table held the reflection of a real shimmering rainbow while people sitting on barstools watched eagerly. Green and white hung everywhere on signs with the name Shamrock Lounge sparkling in gold.

Sonny staggered, in awe of the surroundings. "Wow, this is incredible. Everyone is wearing green. You're right. It is like Saint Patrick's Day at my grandparents' house."

"There're quite a few people here," Jack said, looking in every direction as they passed by a small group. In the corner sat about ten people surrounding a table where someone had made everyone laugh. Jack strained to see the person who'd drawn everyone's attention, but the crowd was blocking whoever it was.

"Come on," she said, looking around the room before pointing to a table next to the juice bar. "Let's go sit over there."

Once they sat down, a woman's voice floated from above them. "How may we serve you?"

Both Jack and Sonny attempted to find the right place to talk into, but there were no microphones anywhere. The voice seemed to be just hovering over them out of nowhere. Finally, Jack decided to just yell out nervously. "Um . . . can I have waffles and sausage with an Island Cream Fiz?"

Sonny looked up and smiled, and then she followed. "And may I have eggs sunny-side up, grilled tomatoes, back bacon, and Irish brown bread? With tea please?" she added.

Not a moment had passed when they looked down and their order had appeared. Jack was staring at a stack of thick golden-brown waffles, plump sausage links, and a bottle of Orange Fiz. A plate of fresh eggs with bright-yellow yolks, thick bacon, fresh brown bread, and bright-red grilled tomatoes along with hot tea appeared in front of Sonny.

Before they began eating, Sonny placed her fork down. With her eyes focused on the orange drink Jack had ordered, she asked, "Jack, what is an Island Cream Fiz?"

"Crap! I completely forgot about that envelope," Jack said, dropping his fork as well.

"What envelope?" Sonny asked.

While they ate, Sonny brought out her pad and pen to make notes of everything Jack was telling her. He went through everything she had missed from the night before—his trip to the shops, including The Candy Garden, following the two attendants, and meeting the fortune teller Luminista and the readings she gave him. Now, with the Orange Fiz drink boosting him up, he rambled on easily about what Luminista had said about the fool card. Lastly, he told her about the envelope with the secret card and the answer to a question he hadn't asked.

Once he finished, Sonny clicked her pen and returned her pad to her pocket. "Almost seems as if you were meant to be here for a reason. Who do you think they were talking about on the seventh floor?"

"I'm not sure," Jack said with his mouth half full of waffles. "They didn't mention a name. Whoever it is apparently was suspected before, and everyone here thinks it's happening again. Wonder if it's the same shadow guy the April Fool was talking about."

"Well, when are you going to check the envelope?" she asked.

"When we finish breakfast, we can check it out," Jack said, cutting into his sausage. "Not sure what good it'll do, though, if we don't understand the cards fully."

As they ate, they debated the meaning of the cards Luminista had read him. It wasn't until after they had finished eating that Jack noticed some familiar people at the juice bar. They were turned around, talking to each other, so he could only view them from behind, but he was sure it was them. Sonny was in the middle of discussing a way to get information when Jack ran over to them excitedly.

"Mom? Dad! I knew you couldn't—" He was cut off mid-sentence when the people, who strongly resembled his parents, turned around. As the woman turned her head, her appearance shifted to a very plump woman covered in pearls and gold and diamond jewelry in a loud orange-and-white dress. The man next to her turned to reveal a much thinner man, who was one-third her size. He wore dozens of ties in various colors around his neck, and he was sitting next to a wheelbarrow full of wrapped gifts. He appeared sullen and had bags under his eyes that were just as heavy as the ones under Jack's.

"Oh, hello, sweetie," she said in a bellowing voice. "It's been some time now since we've had a dreamer. I know you thought I was your mother. Happens to you all when you see us. Stronger when you really miss them, it seems. By the way, you should really tuck in your shirt, honey, and don't slouch."

Jack felt almost heartbroken. Then he noticed Sonny was coming over, so he quickly adjusted his expression. "Why did you look like my parents? And why does everyone here call me a dreamer?"

"Hmm. I thought you'd have figured that out, dear," she said, looking around him. "I'm the Spirit of Mother's Day, honey. You may call me Mother if you'd like, though. Everyone does. So, where's my gift?" she asked, continuing to search, as if he'd hidden it.

"Gift?" Jack asked, "For what?"

"Now, Mother, they're quite young," said the small man Jack assumed was the Spirit of Father's Day. "I'm sure they didn't know."

"You were always so easy on them, Father. I keep telling you that's why you're so shrimpy," stated Mother. "Now, push my gifts from my good children to my room."

"Wait, you haven't told me what a dreamer is," said Jack.

"You didn't bring me a gift, so why should I tell you anything? You don't even love Mother," she said as tears swelled in her eyes and the sound of her shrill crying filled the area. Jack held his ears, looking at Sonny for support, as Mother's crying got louder and more unbearable. Father rolled his eyes, but the other guests ignored it as if it were normal.

"You naughty children are all the same," Mother whimpered. "I suffer for you, try to give you the best, and care for your wellbeing, and I get no appreciation. I could tell the moment you walked over that you don't treat mothers well."

Guilt crept into Jack as he thought about how he'd been treating his own mother. Sonny had brought out her pad and was scribbling something on it. Then she stopped and held up a crude drawing of a bird to her. "Look, I drew you a picture," she said with a smile.

Mother looked up, her tears instantly gone, and she appeared delighted as the crying stopped. "Oh, you do care. When I get home, it's going right on the fridge with the others, sweetie."

It had to be the worst drawing of a bird Jack had ever seen. He wondered how Sonny had been able to make such an accurate drawing of the hotel map. Then Sonny whispered into Jack's ear, "Used to do that for my mom when I was younger."

"So, Mother," Jack said with difficulty, because she was nothing like his mother. "What exactly is a dreamer?"

She was still staring at the picture as if it were an expensive addition to her jewelry collection. "It's not very hard to figure out, really. A dreamer is just someone who can sense things that normally can only be peeked at in their dreams. If you're close enough to a strong source, like this hotel, your spiritual sense becomes active, and you see through the haze to powerful beings . . . like myself." Smiling, she said, "That's why you noticed the repeating days when no one else could."

"Does make sense why I could tell things were wrong before you did, Jack, since I live near here," Sonny said as she wrote in her pad.

"Why is it no one else could sense this place like we could?" Jack asked, keeping track of it all. "And how can I see certain things only through my magnifying glass?" Jack asked, holding up his flashlight. He noticed Father shift uncomfortably and begin fumbling with his ties.

"Well, there are objects that we call totems that make it easier to bend the dreamer's haze and interact with it," Mother said, looking at Father. "Of course, these items are so rare and are really not worth discussing, sweetie."

Jack looked at Sonny, who had stopped writing and was looking from the two spirits to her pen as if connecting dots. "Well, if the days repeat the same way, why did I only meet Sonny a few days ago?"

"No, no. We must be off," Mother said hurriedly. "There are so many gifts I must find storage for. Come now, Father, and don't tangle your ties in the wheels this time."

"Yes, Mother," he said miserably, pushing the wheelbarrow out the doors.

"What do you think that was all about?" Sonny asked as she put away her pen.

"I don't know, but I can tell they're hiding something," Jack responded. "Someone here knows why the days are repeating and about my flashlight."

For a moment, Jack thought about this. Then he started walking, heading toward the exit. "I think I know who might help us."

Sonny followed him out of the lounge, past the guards, who were arguing with a guest that they weren't twins. In the large hall, more attendants were rushing around now. One in particular had an odd expression on her face as she walked by with more yellow tape stuck to her shoe and arms. Jack realized it was Number Forty-Three from the night before. After noticing Jack staring at her, her expression changed quickly to a friendly smile as she resumed her business. Sonny was already on her way to Jack as he hurried to catch up with the attendant.

"Hello, how are you two this morning?" Number Forty-Three asked pleasantly.

"Actually, we have a question to ask you," Jack said, removing the tape from her shoe. "Last night you said you found out what went missing. What happened?"

She froze as if unable to speak. It took a while for her to say anything at all. "I'm really not allowed to say anything about it until the investigation is over," she whispered.

"The investigation?" Sonny asked, "Investigation of what?"

Leaning in closer, Number Forty-Three whispered as quietly as she could. "I really can't tell you what's gone missing, but it's a very important piece. It's the reason why the days are repeating, and if it's not found, it could be a repeat of the dark holiday day."

"What's the dark holiday day?" Jack chimed in.

Number Forty-Three stood back up and resumed her normal tone. "Well, thankfully things really aren't that bad, so no need to worry. Number One has ten floor attendants looking into it and is rejoining us as soon as he returns from seeing the owner. So everything will be taken care of soon. Excuse me, I really must be getting back to my floor."

As they watched her rush off, they decided to focus on getting back to Jack's room and discovering the contents of the envelope. The fountain buzzed with morning colors as they walked by. Orange, yellow, and red water danced in and out of a purple shower resembling the rising sun, and the drops made sounds like birds chirping as Sonny and Jack passed by it on their way to the televator. Once they boarded, Sonny went to press the button to their floor; however, Jack stopped her before she could.

"You have a map in that notepad right?" Jack asked Sonny.

"Yeah, but I don't think it'll be that hard to figure out our floor," answered Sonny.

Jack shook his head. "No, not that. I was thinking about what you said about holiday spirits and the villas. We need to figure out what floor Father's villa would be on?"

She removed the pad from her back pocket, clicked her pen, and flipped through a few pages to the hotel's map. "Okay, how exactly?" she asked.

Immediately, Jack recalled the last time he'd had a normal Father's Day, and he remembered how hard it was this year with his father away. Since he'd been so upset on the first year without him, it wasn't too difficult. "June seventeenth," he said, counting on the map. "So, his villa should be on the twenty-fifth floor."

"How exactly did you figure that out?" asked Sonny.

"My memory's pretty decent for dates," he said with a smirk. He pointed to their floor on the map. "See, when the Spirit of April Fool's Day bumped into us, he was leaving his hidden room behind that wall on the fourteenth floor. With fifty-two floors for the fifty-two weeks of the year, it's easy to figure out it's based on the calendar here. So, if all the rooms are based on days from this year, he would be on the twenty-fifth floor for the—"

"Twenty-fifth week of the year," Sonny finished, pressing the button to the twenty-fifth floor. When they arrived on the new floor, they noticed a significant change in temperature. It was much warmer compared to their floor, but not quite hot. Unlike their hall, this one was designed around the early summer. The smell of freshly mowed grass, swimming pools, and barbecue filled their noses. Seven doors fell against the left side of this hall as well, while a blank wall lay opposite them.

"Alright, it should be right behind this wall," Sonny said, glancing at the drawn map on her pad, then back to the blank area. "So, why are we here?"

"Mother and Father were hiding something," Jack said. He was looking along the blank wall as well. "The way Father was acting makes me think he may be easier to talk to about what's going on." He did not mention that he had no desire to talk to Mother in her frantic mood.

Sonny looked excited. "This could be an interesting story for me to report." She began feeling the wall.

"So, how do you think we get in?" asked Jack, placing his hand against the wall. "Do we just wait until he — Whoa!"

He vanished behind the wall and landed with a thud. Sonny shouted after him, "You alright? I can't get in. It's solid again. What's going on?"

"I don't know, but . . . there's a door here," Jack explained, rubbing his head. "Looks nothing like the other hotel doors. More like a house door, except there's no house. It's just a burgundy door with a key card slot and a light on above it. I really can't see anything else though, it's pitch-black dark. Sort of hard to explain. Be easier if we can get you through too."

Jack reached his hand through the wall, and it appeared on the other side for Sonny to grab. She took it apprehensively, and she was dragged through the wall and onto the other side. "There we go," said Jack.

"Weird. Why couldn't I get through without you?" Sonny asked, looking from the solid wall to Jack.

He shrugged. "Have you tried knocking?"

She could tell from his silence that it hadn't occurred to him yet. She boldly knocked twice on the door, as if it were a normal house, and waited, but there was no answer. She tried twice more, but everything was silent. The light above the door was the only thing that made any movement as she knocked. Jack even tried his key card, but the door rejected it with a soft buzz.

Just as they were about to give up, a voice from behind stirred in the darkness. "May I ask what you two are doing at my door?"

They jumped, startled by the small man standing in the dark behind them. He was without the wheel barrow full of gifts, but his neck was still heavily wrapped with assorted ties. Once they realized it was Father, Sonny spoke. "We came to speak to you and to get more information," Sonny said shakily. "It seemed like you knew more than you were letting on in the lounge."

The look on Father's face was hard to distinguish. Jack wasn't sure if Father was relieved or disappointed, but Jack noticed that he wouldn't look directly at either of them.

"You two are quite observant. Possibly a bit too much so. You know, whether it be candy or knowledge, too much of a good thing can be dangerous. Mother should have never mentioned the totems to you. If this situation is happening again, it could be a dangerous time for us all. You'd be better off left in the dark about this," he stated, weighing out the determination in their faces. "But I have a feeling you won't. I assume you came to ask me about what's in your pocket first?"

Jack felt in his pocket for his flashlight and brought it out. "Yeah, how'd you know?"

"A father's gift," Father said as Sonny began writing again. "But it's not something I'm really at liberty to discuss, so we really should continue inside." Placing his key card inside the door slot, he opened the door. Before Father placed it back into his pocket, Jack noticed a gold star on the card that wasn't on his. Sonny followed Father inside, trailed by Jack, who was still astonished by the unsupported door as he looked inside.

Once through the door, they realized just how large the villas were. They found themselves in what appeared to be the middle of a street in the center of an entire neighborhood. The sun was bright, and the grass was the perfect shade of green on a nice summer day. Beautiful houses aligned both sides of the street as people mowed lawns and children played water games. It resembled a decades-old television program depicting the suburban lifestyle.

"What is this place?" Sonny asked in awe. "How does an entire neighborhood fit here, and who are all these people?"

"Oh, them?" Father responded, leading them to a particularly large house. "Those are the symbols I created to represent Father's day. Loving fathers attending to their families are what I always imagined for the holiday. I spend a lot of free time in my home inventing and tinkering."

Jack became very quiet as they walked across the green lawn to Father's house. It was a brick house with a two-car garage that was a bit larger than the others. He led them inside to the family room, where a few comfortable chairs faced a burning fireplace. It was much cooler inside, but the fire warmed them up quickly. Jack couldn't help but wonder why Father would need a fireplace if it was always summertime, but after mentioning it to Sonny, he assumed it was just his preference. Once they sat down, Father offered them each a Brightberry Fiz. As he drank the purple beverage, Jack tasted a mix of raspberries, grapes, and papaya. Suddenly, he could remember things he hadn't thought of in years as Father sat across from them and asked, "So what did you want to learn from me?"

"Well, for starters, why couldn't Sonny get through the wall without me?" Jack asked.

Father looked into the fire as he pulled a pipe from his pocket. "That would be because of your flashlight. It's stronger than any dreamer's totem I've ever created and has its own special properties."

Jack almost spit out his drink. "Wait, *you* made this?" he asked.

Still staring at the fire, Father continued. "Yes. Before I became a holiday spirit, I made items for an event called The Challenges. Sometimes the items would find their way into your world. While you are here, you are able to do things others can't. And in an experienced hand, it can be a powerful weapon."

The more Brightberry Fiz that Jack drank, the easier he found it to recall things—particularly his dream where he could see a trail through the handle of his flashlight. Sonny seemed to be experiencing similar effects as she recorded everything Father said into her pad quicker than usual.

She spoke next. "We overheard someone talking about a dark holiday? What does it have to do with the repeating days?"

This time, Father turned toward them, but his face was noticeably chalky white as he averted his eyes. "I must explain something else to you, first. When people think of holidays, they don't think of us spirits. We are considered nothing more than a feeling. They actually think of the symbols we've created to aid us. Cupid and Santa Clause are both symbols created by their corresponding spirits." Father stood up and placed a hand on the mantle as he went on. The flames from the fireplace danced on his face. "Over two hundred years ago, a holiday birthed two symbols from his personality. They were brother and sister, and although the sister was quite sweet, the brother was very tricky and very much a jokester. He attempted to create his own dark holiday, whose effects still linger to this day. That almost destroyed everything. Some believe it was the holiday spirit himself who put the symbol up to it. The symbol thought it was all hilarious, of course."

"Who were they?" Sonny asked. Jack had a feeling he already knew.

Father's head slumped further. "The two symbols were from a holiday spirit who spends most of the time locked and secluded at home in the city or here in a villa. As holiday spirits, we are forbidden to speak of this event anymore. The judgment was made that they were innocent, and we must follow that judgment. It's been twelve years since that mess all started with that first great prank. I'm sure you two were too young to remember, but I believe they named it Y2K?"

"How do you know it isn't him now?" Jack asked, thinking about Luminista's judgment card.

Sympathetically, Father explained, "They were proven to have nothing to do with what happened. Yet, what happened was almost tragic. Their aim was completely innocent, as far as we know. If it wasn't for that spirit's role along with the Spirit of April Fool's Day using a trap I created, we may not be having this conversation now."

Jack stopped mid-rebuttal as he realized they weren't talking about the holiday he thought. "Wait, the prankster wasn't the April Fool's spirit? Are you sure?"

Turning toward both of them, Father's face became less pasty. It was the first time they had seen him with even a slight smile. "You mean Barty? Of course not. He's a holiday spirit himself and aided in the capture. I don't believe he even has any symbols. I've known him as long as I've been a holiday spirit. He's purely the do-it-yourself type. I do admit he likes to be in the spotlight, and he is definitely a joker, but truly harmless."

Because she was being so quiet, Jack had forgotten Sonny was even there until she cleared her throat. "So what's going on, now? What is missing?" she asked.

He turned his back to them for a moment and grabbed a drink. It was hard for Jack to remember that Father wasn't his father. When he returned, he sat down and addressed them. "Each holiday spirit is given the honorable duty of protecting their holiday. We receive certain attributes to aid us in this task. There is one holiday spirit that protects an artifact that is used to push time forward. They both disappeared on December twenty-first this year, and their disappearance is the reason the days won't continue."

"Who?" Jack asked desperately. "Who and what went missing?"

"Was it you all those years ago?" asked Sonny. "You act as if you're really upset about it, as if you did it."

With watering eyes, Father attempted to answer their questions, but there was a faint, yet hard knock on the door as the shrill voice of Mother called out. "Father, are you there?" she yelled. "The hotel refuses to build me an automatic gift opener. They claim they don't know how," she scoffed.

"Yes, of course. I'm coming," Father replied.

"How did she get in?" Sonny asked as Father began leading them through a back door. "Your door was locked."

"Oh, she's not inside," Father said miserably. "She's at the first door. I think one of the two things she does well is guilt people with a very loud voice. Believe me, if she had a key, she'd be inside already."

He opened the back door, allowing Sonny out first. He turned around to tell Mother he'd be right there. Being this close to Father when he was not facing him, Jack was overwhelmed by the thought that his father was right in front of him. He could clearly see a perfect resemblance of his father's curly dirty-blond hair and his business suit. Jack grabbed Father around the waist, and a tear ran down his cheek.

"Dad, I knew you couldn't really be dead. Help us so we can get back home. Mom thought I was in denial, but I knew you weren't really gone."

As Father turned around to face Jack, his father's features began to dissolve and the holiday spirit became clearer. Sonny gasped barely as Father placed a consoling hand on Jack's shoulder. "I'm sorry for your loss, son. It was not my intention to confuse you, but you must understand I'm not him."

Taking Jack by the hand, Sonny tried to pull him out of the back door onto the green grass, telling him they had to go, but Jack was still looking at Father with blurry eyes. "I don't know how to solve this," Jack said, unsure who he was talking to now. "What do I do? I need help."

"I apologize, but we don't have much time." Father pointed outside the back door to an open gate. "Follow the path out, and it will lead you to a back door that will lead you back to the hall farther down. . . . You should know I only intended to be an inventor to build great, new things. After this, I won't be able to be contacted any further, or they'll become suspicious."

"You know I don't like to be kept waiting," said Mother, getting louder and more shrill, sounding as if she were about to cry again.

Sonny pulled Jack out past the grass to the open gate as he yelled back to Father. "What do we do to get information if we can't contact you?"

"I'd suggest doing the other thing Mother does well," said Father as he began closing the door, "Order room service."

The last thing they heard as they exited the back door was a loud thud and a man and woman laughing eerily.

# Chapter 5
## The Mighty Pen

As they sprinted back to the hall, everything was a blur to Jack. The time from when they left Father's villa to when they arrived at the back gate melted into an eternity and an instant at once. He wasn't sure how long they had been running through the endless green field, but he knew that sometime after they stopped, Sonny would be asking questions. So he continued at a steady pace, his shoes brushing through the freshly mowed lawn. Traveling through the field, they found a white door in the center, standing alone. As they ran, Sonny said nothing about his reaction to Father and made no eye contact with Jack. This was fine with him as he was in no hurry to bring it up, either. Jack went through the door first, and Sonny followed. They found themselves going through the same blank wall, but on the opposite end of the hall. The smell of mowed grass and swimming pools still lingered in the air.

Jack knew how inquisitive Sonny could be, so before she could ask, he quickly began speaking. "We should probably head back to the room," suggested Jack as he strolled to the televator with his head down.

"What do you mean?" Sonny said, finally looking directly at him. "We should be working on a plan. This could be an amazing case for you and an incredible story for me. I think we should start by asking Manny what he can tell us about the dark holiday and the missing artifact, and then get the information from my room. I stored everything I've written there already," she stated. Her naturally inquisitive demeanor appeared to remerge.

"I don't think it's a good idea to ask the manager," Jack responded. "I doubt he'll be very excited about us interfering, and I don't want any reason for them to keep us here longer. They have the attendants looking into it. I doubt they need our help."

She looked close to mutiny as she prepared her rebuttal. "Well, we have to tell someone, and this all seems rather important to keep to ourselves. We should at least tell Manny or the owner, so we can let them know what Father has told us. I think he is one of the spirits the April Fool's spirit discussed before. Besides, the sooner they find out what's happened, the sooner we can leave, and you may get back to your . . . ," she began, but she stopped short almost after the words were leaving her lips. As she grew quiet, it became awkward before Jack, fighting the urge to protest, agreed to tell the manager, hoping the attention would be off him.

It was almost noon when they took the televator to the ground floor. There were considerably more guests than attendants in the main lobby now; they were coming and going from shops and attractions in the east and west hall. The fountain now sprayed colors of a bright light blue that mimicked the afternoon sky; orange and yellow darted in like rays of sunshine. Number Fifty-Two was still standing where the doorway had been. Now he was directing guests to the various entertainment rooms. Sonny rushed toward him with Jack on her heels, almost colliding with an elderly man. Before they could reach him, the manager, who was dressed in his usual black suit, exited the televator after them. He was dragging a large black plastic bag to a door behind his desk.

Jack tapped Sonny's shoulder and pointed to Emanuel. At once, her path changed and she headed toward the desk. The manager stuffed the bag inside and closed the door, locking it shut. He turned around, startled to find them both waiting at his desk.

"Hello, Manny," Sonny said brightly as she noticed how disheveled his face was. "What happened to you?" she asked. Unlike his usual pristine attire, his face looked as if he had been in a bad fight. Bruises and cuts littered his face like spots on bad fruit, but he spoke as if it didn't bother him.

"Oh, I've been wrestling with all that tape on the first floor and took a nasty fall," he replied in a rush. "Finally got all of it put away, but I still have so much to do."

"Well that's what we wanted to discuss with you," Sonny said, blocking his exit. "We want to help you find out what's going on. We just left Father's villa and received information that could assist in the investigation."

His eyes narrowed, and the bruises around his eyes appeared rougher and tighter. "When were you in Father's villa?" he asked sharply.

It occurred to Jack that Sonny may be incriminating them both. "We met with him earlier to talk about an invention of his," Jack said falsely.

The manager's gaze locked onto Jack's pocket. Part of Jack wondered if he could see the flashlight through his clothes, but he was more worried that Emanuel didn't believe him. "Well, you both have been busy, I can see," Emanuel said, motioning for Number Fifty-Two to join them. "I'm sure you believe you can help, but the owner has directed extra security because of items gone missing. I would say it would be more than dangerous to wander into the villas now, but that would be an understatement. So, let us say you've been warned. Now, I am terribly exhausted by this interference, so I'll have the attendant escort you children to your rooms, where it is safer."

"Children?" protested Sonny, "But we can help you."

Jack whispered to Sonny, "It won't help. Even here, we're just kids to them."

Number Fifty-Two approached them uncertainly. "Yes, Number One?"

"Escort these guests to their rooms and make sure they have everything they need, so they will not disturb anyone else or find themselves in any danger," ordered the manager.

Number Fifty-Two walked with them to the televator and into the hallway of the fourteenth floor. "I do apologize," said the attendant as he marched them out of the televator. "He's been very peculiar since these strange events have gotten closer to the end of the year."

"We could've helped if he'd given us a chance," Sonny said through clenched teeth. "I'm sure we have more information about Father than he realizes."

"Father?" Fifty-Two asked gingerly.

Before getting to his room, Jack stopped the attendant. "Yeah, Father. We were talking to him about . . . an invention a few minutes ago. Why? What's happened?" Jack asked suspiciously.

The attendant appeared cornered, but he tried to maintain his composure. Jack could tell this was difficult for him, because his eyes darted back to the televator. "Well it's really a hotel matter at this point, but it seems everyone tends to find out, and with what's happened, it may be pertinent that you know."

"What has happened?" Sonny inquired.

Number Fifty-Two continued walking to their door as he spoke. "Number One just advised us the Spirit of April Fool's Day has been abducted, and we are now enhancing the hotel security for the villas. The Spirit of Father's Day has gone missing, and there is evidence that leads him to be our primary suspect."

"That's impossible," Jack objected. "We were just there, and he was at breakfast with Mother before that."

"What does Manny plan to do?" Sonny asked.

"Manny?" the attendant asked, stopping at their doors. "Oh, you mean Emanuel? I'm not exactly sure. From what I was informed, they found a hand buzzer piece belonging to the April Fool's spirit there. We usually take matters this important to the owner, but no one's actually seen him leave his room for days now. Recently, he's been phoning in his orders to Number One." He stopped between the two doorways. "If you need anything, don't hesitate to call room service. I'll have lunch sent to you within the hour. Enjoy your stay." He retreated to the televator, leaving them alone.

Glaring at the blank wall across from his room, Jack wondered who would want to abduct the April Fool. He didn't believe he was that annoying, unless someone was tying up loose ends.

*Maybe someone had a motive because of the dark holiday,* he thought. He knew it was possible Father could be involved, but he fully believed that someone was trying to frame him. As he approached the wall, he was tempted to check the villa. He heard Sonny sliding her card into her room slot.

"Manny is being quite ridiculous, but it isn't of much importance right now," she said as she led Jack into the room. "Come inside, I may have an idea."

Sonny's room was much different from what he had expected. Trying to imagine the perfect room for Sonny, it occurred to him that he didn't know the girl who was stuck in the hotel with him very well. There was a basic bed decorated with white-and-black flowers, standard black dressers, and a view of the city much like Jack's. Being so close to noon, the sun peered through the window and magnified the light inside. Everything seemed almost too neat and in its place for someone like her. That was, until his attention was directed to the walls. A soothing eggshell white had been shocked by a rainbow splash of colored writing covering the walls. Every detail she had written in her pad appeared to be rewritten there in different colors. It included the first time she'd met Jack, the flat tire on his mother's car, and the eight repeating days she had experienced. The detailed notes and descriptions flowed around the room like a rainbow.

"This must've taken you hours to rewrite," Jack said in disbelief. As he walked around her room, he noticed paragraphs about her mother being gone, how she enjoyed art class at school, and being ignored by her father at home.

"Actually, no, I didn't have to," Sonny responded, holding up her red-and-silver pen. "I wasn't sure if I should tell you or not when we first met, but after what Father said about your flashlight and the totems . . . well, there may be another reason we met."

He examined the pen curiously. "What's so special about it?"

"My grandfather left it to me with no instructions of how to use it. Just to explore the world through my own eyes and write my story as I see it. Well, the first thing I noticed was, for starters, anything I write with it appears on the walls here and disappears from my pad. I never have to turn a page," she said, observing his reaction. "It was fairly odd the first time I used it."

"Has it always done that?" he asked as he looked around at all the notes she had taken.

"Not exactly," she said, sitting on a desk chair. "That only started when we came to the hotel. See, my grandfather and I really got along well, because he was a writer. When he passed it to me, I was much younger. And anytime I would write something, it would appear in my journal at home. It was hard to get used to it. Every school test I took would go straight to my journal. After a few weeks, I discovered it depends on the clicks."

Holding the pen and pad up to Jack, she clicked it twice. The words dissolved from the walls, leaving them blank, and reported back to the paper. Each month's notes were written in a different color, reminding him of the fountain on the fifty-second floor. Shades of brown represented November notes, while December was colored in forest green. She clicked it once, and the words vanished from the pad and returned to the walls.

"That's amazing," Jack said. He was astounded, wondering now what other hidden mysteries his flashlight may have.

"You haven't seen the best part," Sonny declared. "If I can't remember what I've written, then I click three times and ask a question."

After scribbling on the page, she held up the pad with the question *what is my birthday?* written on it. Immediately, the answer *April 29th* appeared and then disappeared. "Unfortunately, it can only answer questions from what I've written, but it gave me an idea. We can call room service like Father suggested and simply ask what we need to know."

Bringing up Father compelled Jack to relive what had happened earlier. Sonny seemed to read his troubled demeanor. "Are you alright?" she asked.

"Yeah, it sounds like a good plan, and we might be able to clear Father's name," Jack uttered sullenly.

"No, I mean about your father?" Sonny asked delicately, attempting to not upset him. "Until recently, I assumed your parents were divorced. You were saying you were going to see your father?"

For a while, neither of them said a word. Fearing she had crossed the line, Sonny seemed ready to change the subject when he took a deep breath. "We were on our way to see him, because December twenty-first is his birthday. It was Christmas time about a year ago. My dad was away on business in Tokyo, presenting blueprints," Jack explained shakily, reliving the period. "He wasn't sure if he would make it back for Christmas, but I was being stubborn. Weeks had passed without seeing him. Mom and I both missed him. After a while, when he called, I started ignoring it. I remember the gifts from my mom and the gift I'm trying to get to him now sitting under the tree. I worked so hard on it, and it made me furious he wouldn't be there for it. I blamed him for not being around and breaking all the promises he'd made lately."

"What happened?" Sonny asked after he paused.

Turning his head to hide his face, Jack continued his story. "My mom and I had no idea, but he had convinced his boss that everything else could be done from home and gotten permission to fly back as soon as possible. Police said the storm was completely unexpected. It was supposed to be clear skies. After the lightning struck the plane, people were pretty banged up. But everyone survived, except for him. We found out the next day, after the wreckage was cleared. He was the last man on the plane after it blew. The passengers said he left his phone on the plane and heard the phone ringing. From what they said, he thought it was me. He ran back to get it apparently, but there was a gas leak. And it blew. The police from the station he had built let us know after it happened."

When Jack told this story, most people would apologize. That was one of the reasons he didn't like telling the story. No one understood that the gesture was appreciated, but an apology for something they had no control over never made sense to him. It almost made him angry that they seemed to think it would bandage the hurt. However, Sonny didn't apologize. As usual, she was more curious than anything.

"I don't understand," Sonny said gingerly. "I thought he brought you the flashlight as a gift?"

"At the time, I had no idea what his plan was, but before we talked, he had sent me a gift through the mail, thinking he wouldn't make it back," Jack stated, holding his flashlight. "That's why he called. But I didn't give him a chance to tell me. Strange thing is, I don't remember much from that day after what happened. I don't remember calling him back or what I did that day now. At the time, all I cared about was getting more than a phone call from him. And if I hadn't pushed him to make the flight. . . . I'd do anything to hear him call now."

The room was still. Jack's quietness implied that he was done discussing it, but Sonny's feedback was unusual. "I'm surprised you weren't writing this down," he said finally, a little choked up.

Sonny grinned. "Your life is not my story to write." She made her way to the room phone and glanced at the long list of service numbers. Several services were available to call, including the kitchen, a salon, the manager, information, and even a pet groomer. Oddly enough, room service was listed for each one, but with no number.

She picked up the phone and listened, but there was no sound — no dial tone or operator. A few more seconds passed. Still, no one said a word on the other end. "There's no one there. I don't understand. How did Father expect us to get information about the hotel with the phones not working?" she asked Jack.

A profound knock echoed from the door. Sonny hung up the phone immediately. Her gaze shifted from the door and back to Jack. His attention was focused on the open space at the bottom of the door as he looked for either a silhouette or some kind of clue as to who was behind it. However, nothing seemed to move on the other side.

"Would you like to get it?" Sonny asked.

"It's your room." He sighed reluctantly. "Fine, I'll see who it is." Cautiously, he walked up to the door and looked through the peephole, but no one was around. He grabbed the handle and opened the door slowly, looking around. The entire floor appeared to be empty. The only thing he found was a gleaming gold tray with a book entitled *A Historical Look at the Holiday Hotel* along with a card below him. Jack picked up the book and card and closed the door hastily.

"So?" Sonny asked. "Who was it?"

"The card says 'thank you for your order,'" Jack responded, continuing to direct his stare at the book. "I think it's the information you ordered."

Taking the book from Jack, Sonny brought out her pad and pen. "Well, they're quite prompt, aren't they? I rarely have a reason to use this. Hope it works on a book this big." Writing the word *copy* in large letters on the pad, she placed the book atop it. Pages of the book ruffled from the top down to the pad like a wave, and a moment later it lay still again. After removing the book from the pad, she tossed it onto the bed. Her writing dissolved, and her pad was blank once again.

"That's perfect. Now, we should be able to just ask what we need to know," Jack said, pacing along the bed.

"That's what I hope," Sonny said, sitting on the floor as if preparing to study. "So, what's first?"

"I have an idea already." Jack stopped pacing. "But first, ask it who's staying in the villa on the first floor."

She wrote down the question, and as requested, the pad responded promptly with pages of information.

"The first floor of the Holiday Hotel holds the villa of the protector of sands, the holiday spirit of New Year's Eve. With the placement of this villa, the floor itself has the unique property of dimming or brightening, depending on its closeness to the end of the year. Since the hotel was established, this villa has been the home of the transitional event that brings the end of one year to the beginning of the next. During this time, the celebration of the New Year's spirit's death and rebirth to his new body is observed. This is the only time the spirit is seen until the last day of the following year."

Jack reread it several times before asking Sonny his second question. "Can you ask it about the Spirit of New Year's itself?"

Sonny asked the next question, and the pad answered instantly.

"With the nature of his rebirth, the Spirit of New Year's is unique. This spirit has a life span of one year. He ages from an infant on the first day of every year, and dies on the last. From that death, the cycle begins again with his birth. Because he shares these traits in common with the mythical bird that bursts into flames at its death and is reborn from the ashes, he commonly goes by the name Phoenix.

The Spirit of New Year's has had many notable accomplishments, including his part in the capture of the Loch Ness Monster. However, his primary role as a holiday spirit is to protect the arcane sands, the most important of which is the Infinite Hourglass."

"Wait, the Infinite Hourglass?" Jack said immediately. "With all the days repeating at home, that's gotta be what's missing. We need to find out more about the hourglass."

Sonny had already finished asking what the Infinite Hourglass was. "I am way ahead of you," she said as the writing appeared on the pad.

"The Infinite Hourglass is possibly the most important item currently held within the walls of the Holiday Hotel. The arcane sands contained within this hourglass control the transition of time. Normally, an item such as this would be hidden away inside one of the hotel's secure safes, where it could be guarded at all times. However, the hourglass must be held within range of the spirit's throne, becoming its transmitter by the end of each day. Without its correct placement, the day will continue until the intended last moment of the year approaches, at which point all time will become still indefinitely."

"Indefinitely?" Sonny asked as she finished reading. Searching the room, she found a clock with a date displayed. "If the days have repeated eight times for me, and we have been here one, that leaves us a little under a day and a half before the end of the thirty-first."

Jack twirled his flashlight between his fingers as he so often did when he was thinking. "Okay, I may have a plan. But I need you to ask the pad about the dark holiday first."

After writing the question, she looked up at him with disappointment. "It says there's no information found. Maybe it didn't occur here in the hotel. What about that spirit everyone suspects besides Father? Maybe if we can get into his room?"

Jack shook his head. "The April Fool mentioned the spirit Mr. Shadow, remember? It could be him, but we have to figure out what floor he'd be on. . . . " Jack paused for a moment and thought back. "The floor attendant mentioned a couple floors . . . when I heard Fifty-Two and Forty-Three talking last night, she mentioned one because she was glad she was on the floor above his. A spirit that was involved in the dark holiday is there."

"So it's on that floor, which was the week of what holiday? Halloween, I think." Sonny wrote in the holiday as she concluded.

"Only thing is, we don't know is if he's really involved. And even if we did, we still have no way in." Jack continued to pace. He was about to sit onto the bed when Sonny had a thought and stood from the floor. "We need a way to find clues, but the only real crime scene is the New Year's spirit's villa, and we have no way in."

"Well, remember how Father used his key card to get inside his villa?" she asked Jack.

"Yeah, it had a gold star or something on it," Jack remembered, looking at his own blank key card.

"I have a plan to get into the villa, but we need a way to get a key card for the room," Sonny said, making her way to the phone. "So, I figured we could just call room service for a key card." She picked up the phone and asked for a universal key. They waited for the knock on the door, but nothing happened. After asking for every type of key to open the villa, she turned to Jack in defeat. "Doesn't seem to be working."

Strolling over to her as she held the phone, Jack searched through the list of available services. "It won't work. I just remembered Fifty-Two mentioning only the owner and Emanuel had access to all the rooms. Maybe we could call for the owner, but only he would be able to get us a skeleton key."

At once, another knock hit the door. This time, Sonny dropped the phone and rushed over to the door to find a gold tray. It held a key card with a small black skull marked on it. Taking the key back inside, she left the tray and shut the door.

"Well, took long enough," she said with frustration.

"That doesn't make any sense," Jack explained as he examined the new key card Sonny held. "If the manager and the owner are the only ones who have access to all the rooms, why would they send one to us? Unless there's something I misheard."

As Jack considered the reasons behind their entrance into the hotel, Sonny recognized something on the back of the information book. "Hey, Jack. What's your middle name?"

"Umm. Eli," Jack responded, unsure why she had asked.

She wrote on her pad, asking who the owner of the hotel was. It responded exactly as she expected. She gestured to the book and her pad on the bed. "You should probably see these." She was staring at a picture of a plaque depicting the hotel on the back cover of the book. It was the same plaque they had witnessed when they came into the hotel. Jack had thought it read "JET Enterprises," but it was in fact plated with "J.E.T. Enterprises." "Those are your initials. I asked the pad who the owner was and got the same answer."

"That could explain how we got inside after Number Fifty-Two sealed the door," Jack muttered to himself. He racked his brain as Sonny created her own conclusion. "But why wouldn't it let us leave? Not that it would matter now. If we don't solve this case, it's all over anyways. I don't think we really tried to leave, did we?"

"I believe I know what happened," she stated confidently. "Clones."

Jack looked back up to her, and assumed he had heard her mistakenly. "Did you say clones?" he asked, remembering her alien theory.

She nodded with the pen in her mouth as she brought her pad back out. "They must have cloned you and wiped your memory of it before your clone became owner of the hotel. That would explain why it has your initials for the owner."

"I doubt I was cloned," Jack stated, half amused. "This is a hotel for spirits, not *clone* spirits. And Emanuel said we are still alive. Plus, if I was the owner, they'd have to take orders from me, and we wouldn't still be here right now. Besides, how could I be the owner when we just got here?"

"I suppose that makes sense." Sonny's disappointment was apparent. "So, how would you explain it all? How is it you could order this key, and I couldn't?"

"Well, since I'm not a spirit, I don't see how I could really own this hotel. Especially since I know I never built it," Jack concluded somberly. "A few of the attendants said I looked familiar. I brushed it off at first, but now I know why. My guess would be the owner would be able to build this place if he were an architect. Mostly, I know it's not me, because the plaque isn't named after me." Jack thumbed through the book. After searching the glossary, he held the book open to a page and pointed to a portrait of a man under the chapter about the founders. It pictured an older gentleman in his forties with short, curly blond hair and pearl-brown eyes just like Jack's. "I'm Jack Eli Taylor, *Junior*, which means, somehow, the owner of the hotel is my father."

# Chapter 6
## *Sands & Hourglasses*

Cold winds whisked past Jack's face with the same force they had when he'd entered the rest area. They arrived on the first floor, and Jack was forced to tighten his grip on the leather coat covering him. They were unable to pull up any information about the owner from the book or the pad, but if the owner really was his father, he had hope that he'd be able to speak to him once more. So, after eating the lunch Number Fifty-Two had sent up, they snuck into the televator and headed up to the top floor. Once they had left, Jack became less thrilled about Sonny's plan to investigate the New Year's spirit's villa. She, on the other hand, didn't appear bothered by the plan or the wind. She continued on as usual with her pad and pen, ready to report whatever may come next without a single shiver or cold chill.

It was very dark, just as the history book had described it would be. The floor was noticeably getting darker as time went on, as if the setting sun were right outside the hall. The darkness followed the moments before the end of the year. Bringing out the skeleton key card, Jack turned on his flashlight to pierce through the darkness and witnessed the hall in its light. Even though Sonny was with him, the hall appeared more desolate than any other they had been to yet, as if they were the last guests at a finished party. Besides the cold winds and their footsteps, the loud ticks from six clocks measuring time in unison were the only sounds. Confetti and the red, purple, yellow, and green balloons decorating the doors failed to raise the cheerfulness of the hall. Like the other floors, seven rooms stretched across the left wall opposite a blank one. But between each of these rooms was a basic black-and-white office clock. The same time showed on each clock as it ticked away, getting closer to one o'clock.

"We should go to the middle of the wall," suggested Sonny. Jack aimed his flashlight at the center of the blank wall. The light shined through the wall, displaying an archway leading to a steep staircase. "Look," Sonny said in awe. "I think it's your flashlight that is bending the haze of the wall."

Sonny led inside, climbing through the lit wall without the need to touch Jack. It wasn't long before she noticed something different. "Strange," she said as she stepped inside where the light displayed. "The door is already open."

Looking around the archway as he followed, Jack appeared to have just realized this as well. "Attendants probably left it open," he said, shivering. "I doubt anyone dangerous would be up there now." The cold made it difficult to concentrate, and the situation made him uneasy. "We should be careful, though. There may be someone else up there still investigating. Getting caught by Emanuel or an attendant won't help us get answers."

Since he carried the only light, Jack led the way up the narrow, steep staircase to the roof. The higher they climbed, the colder and darker it seemed to become. Several minutes passed by and neither of them spoke. Jack began to wonder how anyone could steal anything, especially a spirit, and get away with it here. The stairs creaked loudly, and because there were so many of them, it seemed impossible not to be caught running down the only exit.

With the light pointing to the ground to show where he was stepping, Jack was caught off guard by the staircase's ceiling as he ascended. Taking another step up caused him to hit it hard. "Ouch!" he bellowed sharply, rubbing the top of his head.

After almost losing her footing from running into him, Sonny attempted to peer around him in the narrow staircase to no avail. "What did you hit?" she asked, looking up.

"The ceiling, but I think it may be a door." Jack pointed his flashlight at the dark surface as he searched for a handle. The rough edge of metal reflected the light from the flashlight. Jack squeezed the handle and pushed the door open. The staircase was engulfed by the bitter winter winds. Up the last few steps, Jack and Sonny found their way to the large landing atop the roof of the hotel. Leaving the darkness, it was the first time they had been outside since they had arrived. The darkness of the staircase made it difficult for their eyes to adapt to the bright light outside as it reflected off a delicate layer of snow.

The view from the roof was breathtaking after being locked away from the outside for so long. The city was too far below to be seen properly, but the rays from the sun blocked most of the view anyway. A few birds flew by, apparently unaware the building existed. A dance floor half the size of a football field stretched across the extensive roof. Tables and chairs were scattered about, overturned by a scuffle. Deflated balloons hung from walls and swayed in the air, and broken glass from clocks sat stacked in a pile.

"Someone must have left in a rush," Sonny said. Removing her pen and pad from her pocket, she made her way to the middle of the roof. Jack moved forward to examine the door itself and then scanned the floor, stepping onto a piece of sticky yellow tape. He realized how much tape still filled the edges of the room and had been tracked throughout the room by the attendants. Removing the tape from his shoe, he found a broken mechanical button with two wires that he somewhat recognized but couldn't recall where or why. It was clear and the letters *LR* were engraved on it in white. Placing it into one of his coat pockets, he continued on.

The wreckage was difficult to sift through. Sonny walked around, making notes of it all, as Jack tried to find anything that may be helpful. Carefully stepping over broken champagne glasses and tablecloths stuck to tape, Jack found an elegant crimson robe bundled up against a wall. There was nothing inside it, but it seemed fancy, as if it belonged to someone important. A few minutes later, they made their way to the opposite end of the room, where a tall throne sat. It was silver with red plush inserts for the back, bottom, and armrests. Jack inspected it, trying to remember what he had learned earlier about the Spirit of New Year's and the hourglasses, but he found nothing to connect the two.

After searching most of the room, he found nothing else. The book had mentioned several other arcane hourglasses, but neither he nor Sonny found any at all. The only sign of them he did find was a shelf above the throne with an infinity symbol below it. Jack squatted down to look underneath and around the throne with the light of his flashlight. Once his search was finished with no result, he signaled Sonny, who had just finished writing her last entry.

"So have you found anything worth noting?" she asked.

"Not exactly, no." Jack got up and turned his flashlight off. "What do you remember about the other hourglasses? I haven't seen any anywhere, but I was hoping to get a look at one, so we'd have an idea what we're looking for. It could be a lot bigger or smaller than we realize."

"Maybe they were moved so no one could take them, too?" Sonny suggested.

"You're probably right," Jack agreed. He was taking a step backward to get a better look at the throne and wall when he stumbled over a chair lying on its side. He dropped his flashlight; it rolled to the side of the throne and stopped.

"You okay?" Sonny asked. "Or is this a new habit of yours to fall over things when I'm around?"

Regaining his composure, Jack sat up. "Yeah, I'm fine. Just need to look before I fall off a cloud."

Sonny was bending over to pick up Jack's flashlight when she noticed something sparkly next to the chair. "Jack, you should see this," she said, pointing down.

Peering through the magnifying glass, Jack viewed the sparkling crystals inside a glass container. Switching to looking through the area above the eyepiece, he observed the still-bare wall. When he looked through the handle again, something appeared behind it at every glance, reminding him of the trail in his dream a few nights before.

It was difficult to focus as he shook from the cold, but he held his arm steady as he held the flashlight handle up to his eye. He could see an entire wall of hourglasses filled with sparkling sand. Each container was a different size. The rows of shelves stretched from one side of the wall to the other. Some hourglasses were as small as a soda can, but others were as large as a car battery. Each one was labeled in a marking Jack didn't understand. Scanning the shelf above the throne, Jack discovered another hourglass; it was filled with funneling black sand. It was slightly larger than any of the others, and looking inside was like staring at a contained void. He handed the flashlight to Sonny and pointed to the shelf.

"Well, if that's the Infinite Hourglass, why are the days still repeating?" Sonny asked, reaching up to it.

"I don't think it is," Jack responded. "That hourglass is above the symbol. I'm fairly sure whoever's holding Phoenix has the hourglass, too. Only explanation why they're both missing, but there is something definitely eerie about this one."

Sonny reached for the black-sand hourglass, but her hand began shaking violently. She felt a jolt through her fingers, and a shock surged through her body.

"What happened?" Jack asked, shivering.

"I'm alright, I think," Sonny said, holding her hand and backing away. "It just shocked me." Her hand began to swell slightly, and a few of her paper-cut wounds began to reopen. She hastily took a bandage from her side pocket and wrapped it without wincing much and continued on.

"There must be something protecting it," Jack stated, examining her hand. "We should get going in case someone comes up. . . ." He stopped as he noticed a sparkling tan trail through his magnifying glass that traced a path throughout the room. "You should take a look at this," he said to Sonny.

Looking through the handle, she followed the trail as it led back to the staircase leading downstairs. "Looks like brighter sand, but anyone could have left it. It's everywhere here." She handed the flashlight back to him.

"I thought about that, but there's only one set of footprints in it besides ours," Jack replied, bending down to touch the sand. Relieved he wasn't shocked by it like Sonny had been, he sniffed it and immediately began to yawn before she suggested they leave. Taking a last look outside, they exited the roof and climbed back down the steep stairs, following the trail. It became noticeably warmer as they descended. The stairs creaked with each step as they hurried down. It wasn't until they reached the base of the stairs again that something seemed off. Chills crept up Jack's spine, and he could tell Sonny felt it too. He could also tell it wasn't from the cold.

"What is that?" he asked.

Before she could reply, the televator lit up in blue and the bell rang. Jack stood frozen, unsure what to do. He was confident they were caught with nowhere to run. Going back up the stairs to the villa would make them appear suspicious at the crime scene. Yet standing on the first floor when they were supposed to be in their own rooms wouldn't look much better, especially to the manager. To his relief, Sonny had taken the skeleton key card from him before he knew it and opened the door to room number three, pulling him inside with her. He tripped over the threshold as she closed the door gently, leaving a small gap open for them to see through.

Stumbling inside, Jack thought it lucky that the room wasn't occupied, but he had to take in its emptiness. It hadn't been set up at all yet. The walls were pure white and bare, no closets or restrooms existed, and besides a small lamp on the floor, there was nothing inside. It was more like the beginning stages of a cartoon than a hotel room.

"Why is it you're always pulling me through doors?" Jack asked, recovering from his stumble. "You know, that's what brought us here to begin with."

"Shhh," she whispered, looking through the door crack. Watching the televator open, she witnessed a tall figure wearing a dark suit and red tie exit into the hall. A black fedora-style hat hid his face in shadow. As he passed room three, the lights of the clocks dimmed as if afraid to shine too brightly on him. The slow steps he took made it appear as if he were gliding over the floor instead of walking.

"I think it's Mr. Shadow," Sonny said, watching him walk to the center of the hall. He turned toward room three, and although she couldn't see his face, Sonny was fairly certain he knew she and Jack were there. Chills engulfed the atmosphere, and Jack began experiencing dormant fears he hadn't felt in years. Images of creepy clowns laughing maniacally when he was four and a vicious dog snarling and chasing him at seven all came rushing back to him at once. He could tell Sonny was feeling the effects as well, but he wasn't sure what she was imagining as she closed her eyes tightly.

Just as suddenly as the numbing fears had appeared, they began to subside. Mr. Shadow had turned his attention to the staircase through the haze of blank wall and quickly disappeared behind it. The echo of his slow footsteps became softer as he went. The gentle glow of the clocks seemed to brighten a bit. As this seemed the best time to get back to their rooms, Sonny waved for Jack to follow. She handed him his key card and led the way out of the room to the televator. As they left, he used his flashlight to follow the trail, which appeared to lead out to the televator.

"It's gonna be a dead end," he said as he pressed the button to the fourteenth floor. "There's no way we'll figure out what floor the trail leads to without checking each floor, and that could take hours with so many floors. We'll have to save that as a last resort or check a primary suspect, if needed."

As they traveled to the fourteenth floor, Sonny told Jack what she'd seen Mr. Shadow doing. Jack wondered what information the book would have on the spirit, but Sonny's attempts to ask her pad proclaimed no response, just as it had for the dark holiday.

"There's still no information on him, no matter how I ask." She stared at the blank pad.

"Mr. Shadow must have something to do with the dark holiday," Jack pondered to himself as they reached Sonny's room. "But the holiday spirit from the dark holiday had twin symbols. What symbols has Halloween ever had? This isn't adding up, but he's obviously being suspicious." As they entered her room, Sonny sat on the bed and mentioned something about ordering another book, but Jack's attention was elsewhere. "I think we should talk to the spirits of the holidays that occurred closest to the repeating days. If we can find out anything unusual that may have happened near that time, we could get closer to finding the right hourglass. What holiday just passed that you can remember, Thanksgiving?"

"There may be some I don't know of, but my neighbor had a menorah lit for Hanukkah," Sonny said, thinking back. "I thought I heard of something called a Forefathers' Day, but I'm not sure. Then Christmas, I suppose, would have been next. This week, correct?"

"We should check the map for those holidays, then," he said from the door way. "I've got to go to my room and get my book of clues."

"Book of clues," she said, stifling a yawn. "For what?"

"When we were upstairs, I didn't see any damage on the doors, handles, locks, or hinges," Jack said as he was backing out. "I'm pretty sure there was no break-in. My guess is the Spirit of New Year's let someone into his villa, probably someone he trusted. And they took him. Whoever it was must have returned, looked for the hourglass, and trashed the room in the process. And then I found this." Jack held up the mechanical part he'd found. "I'm not sure what it is, but it looks familiar. I have a book to help decipher clues in my room. I'll get it and be right back."

After exiting the room, he used the key card and entered his room, but something had changed. His room had the same atmosphere as the New Year's spirit's villa. The television was on the ground and had a gaping hole in the screen. His bed had been overturned along with the mini fridge and dressers. His clothes were thrown everywhere and turned inside out, as if someone had searched the pockets. The case for his flashlight had been destroyed altogether, and he wasn't sure where the book was now. He couldn't tell where anything was now because of the mess.

Immediately, he closed the door and rushed back to Sonny's room to tell her what had happened and to make sure she was alright. Her room had appeared normal a moment ago, but the thought of someone lurking in the restroom or under her bed suddenly plagued his mind, and he hoped someone wasn't in there with her. He knocked repeatedly on her door, calling out her name, but she didn't answer. Banging as hard as he could, he was sure he heard someone make a sound inside, but, still, no one answered. It sounded almost as if someone were snoring.

Finally, as he was about to run for help, he remembered the skeleton key card in his pocket. He opened her door as fast as he could, bracing himself for whoever may be inside. She lay very still on the bed, snoring softly. Surveying the room, he didn't find anyone inside, except her. He didn't find anyone in the restroom or under the bed, and her room looked just as abnormal as it had looked before—tidy, but with words covering the walls.

"Why wouldn't you answer?" Jack asked, approaching her. "Someone trashed my room. I thought they might be in here with you."

Sonny didn't answer. Jack wasn't sure if she was listening at all and began shaking her. With the exception of the paper cuts on her fingers, no other marks or scratches seemed to afflict her. As he shook her, her heavy breaths became more apparent, and after a moment, he grasped that she was deeply asleep.

It didn't make any sense. He had walked away for only a moment, but Sonny appeared to be in a deep Sleeping Beauty state. He wasn't sure if someone had drugged her or not, but he knew there had to be a reason his room currently had the worst housekeeping ever. From the corner of his eye, he noticed a small sign on the nightstand that drew his attention away.

*Don't worry about a good night's sleep ever
again. Each bed set at the hotel is made of the perfect
material and is tailored to you. It's the right softness
and thickness to make you believe you've slept on a
cloud. To make sure you'll get at least eight hours of
rest, we've sprinkled a diluted dream dust made from
arcane sands. Lie down and inhale to be asleep in
moments. Enjoy your stay.*

As he read it, one of the two events became clear. His room was still a wreck, but Sonny was only asleep because of the bed. Relieved she wasn't hurt, Jack took her by the shoulders and placed her on the floor, hoping that removing her from the bed would wake her up. To his disappointment, there was no change, and she snored just as loudly and lay just as limply as before. He imagined that she must have already inhaled this dream dust, so he went to the phone to ask for help. Meanwhile, Sonny turned over, pulling a blanket onto the floor.

"I need help," Jack said into the receiver. "My friend's asleep because of this dream dust, and she won't wake up."

A knock echoed on the door almost immediately. Jack was still holding the phone when he heard it and exchanged a look between the door and the phone before rushing to it. He expected to find an attendant or the manager. Instead, all he found was another gleaming gold tray. The hall was empty as if whoever knocked had instantly vanished. This time, only a white card was placed on the tray with a message: *Thank you for your order. Please report to the 7th Floor, Room 14.*

# Chapter 7
## *The Love Doctor*

Through Sonny's window, Jack could see the sun's declining arc into the west. The day was now three-quarters complete, and he was running out of time. Although he had learned the layout of the hotel well enough, he felt lost without his partner completely conscious. Her head slumped over his shoulder like a sack as he half-carried her to the televator, hoping he didn't run into anyone. Leaving her in the room and bringing help back seemed like an easier plan, but after someone had broken into his room, Jack didn't believe that her room would be any more secure.

Leaning her inside the televator as he pressed the button for the seventh floor, his thoughts drifted back to his demolished room. He hadn't stayed long enough to think much about it, but it resembled the wreckage of the New

Year's spirit's villa more than he realized. He was sure the culprit was looking for something. At this point, he just hoped it wasn't him the intruder was after.

Arriving on the seventh floor, Jack shouldered Sonny and proceeded into the hall. After receiving his order from room service, he was fairly certain whom he was sent to see since the floors were based on the weeks of the year. He couldn't help but recall what the attendant had said to Number Fifty-Two about the possibility of a holiday spirit on the seventh floor being involved. But he found himself with limited options to help Sonny.

After seeing the red and pink hearts attached to long-stem roses draped over each archway, he was sure whom he was going to see. The doors were decorated to resemble chocolate hearts. Throughout the hall, colorful bubbles hovered in the air, and sweet smells like the ones from The Candy Garden filled his nose. Overwhelmed by the sickeningly sweet hall, Jack quickly took Sonny to the middle of the wall and used his flashlight to find the door behind the wall's haze. A stand-alone door appeared just as one had appeared in the other villas, but this one was bright red with a silver heart-shaped knocker in the center. Approaching it cautiously, he used the knocker a few times and then waited for a response. However, when Sonny began drooling on his shoulder, Jack became impatient and used the skeleton key card to access the villa.

The open door unveiled an immense garden of tall green-leaved trees and rose hedges dusted with a light mist of snow under a shining sun. Unlike Father's villa of homes, no other people seemed to be around this one. A gray stone road covered the ground where marble fountains, ancient roman pillars, wooden benches, and several statues stood.

The statues were noticeably larger than an average-sized person. Roman warriors armed with sword and shield stared menacingly at passersby as if they were ready to leap from there podiums and attack at any moment. The lengthy path curved its way to a large red-brick storybook-style home with grand windows and white shutters shaded under multiple wide black roofs.

The home conveyed an inviting impression, and Jack was convinced it would be the best place to search for help. Considering the constraints of time and believing they were in a safe area, he decided it would be faster to continue to the house alone. He laid Sonny down onto a bench, and as she turned over comfortably, he began walking down the stone path toward the house.

Rose bushes growing at the sides of the path held large softball-sized buds in many colors. The thorns looked razor sharp and seemed to be pointing directly at Jack as he proceeded forward. Although no one was around, he became more aware of another presence, and Jack turned quickly after hearing a crumbling sound like footsteps on gravel. The motionless eyes of every statue standing on a pedestal seemed to be set on him as he passed. At first thought, he put it off as an illusion, like portraits whose eyes follow you. Walking a few paces farther, he heard another noise much like wind through leaves, and almost at once, he felt something whizzing past his ear.

Before he knew it, the Roman statues were moving, climbing down from their pedestals and marching toward Jack with shields up and swords drawn. The rose bushes were suddenly larger and fully bloomed, and they were now shooting sharp thorns from their vines. He was tempted to run back to the entrance, but he realized how much closer the house was. As it was, they all appeared to be after him and to be ignoring Sonny, and he didn't want to bring any attention to her. So Jack ran toward the house as fast as he could, dodging arrows that hissed with pink smoke like venomous serpents. Thorns hitting the ground were eating away at the stone, leaving melted puddles of rock and dirt. Rolling between the legs of one of the statues with hearts on its biceps, he avoided an arrow aimed at him that struck the large statue instead. A small explosion blew the warrior's shoulder and arm off and was followed by the sound of crumbling rock. The blast propelled Jack sideways with force into a pink rose bush.

Regaining his balance, Jack saw that his hand was bleeding from a small stinging cut. Shaking his hands, he tried to go forward but was barely able to move his legs. They became heavy as if the gravity had been increased severely. He could feel something coursing through his veins as he tried to proceed. His arms felt stiff, as if they were being glued in place. Soon, his entire body was paralyzed. Blurry figures of statues approached, but he was unable to see straight. At once, he collapsed, completely motionless, into the dirt with a hard thud. The ringing of an alarm sounded. Except for the clearing dust cloud created by his fall, the last thing he saw before his eyes finally shut fully was a blurry white-coated figure running up to him.

Subtle music from a piano playing awoke Jack abruptly, and he tried to sit up. His vision was still pretty fuzzy, as if he'd been asleep for too long. Assorted plant species he didn't recognize hung from the ceiling in blue pots, strongly reminding Jack of a rainforest. After rubbing his eyes, he placed a hand onto the white sheet he had woken up on and found himself on top of a hospital gurney, but he didn't appear to be in a hospital. Instead, he was in the middle of an elaborate eggshell-white kitchen, complete with cinnamon-colored marble countertops, a refrigerator, and chrome fixtures. It wasn't long before he became aware that he was inside the house from the trail, but a few things seemed out of place. A teapot bellowed teal steam. Vials holding what seemed to be twitching vines were lined up against a counter. And he noticed a glass jar above the cupboard in front of him. At first, he thought it may have been his eyes still adjusting and playing tricks on him, but he panicked when he saw the beating heart inside the jar. Checking to make sure it wasn't his, he felt for any missing body parts, but he was fairly sure he was still intact.

He wondered what had happened to Sonny. He tried to remember how he had gotten there, but it was all pretty spotty. Thoughts of Sonny either back on the bench or possibly experiencing a similar fate developed in his mind as he tried to think of a way out. His jacket lay next to him along with his key card, but he knew something was wrong when he couldn't find his flashlight.

Footsteps echoed from another room, growing louder, as if someone were on the way in. Jack searched the counter and his pockets for his flashlight but still couldn't find it. Rummaging for a handle behind him, he pulled open a few drawers. Behind spoons, tongs, and a pizza cutter, he found vials of brown-and-green liquid. Removing one from the drawer, he held it up, ready to throw, as the door swung open.

Yawning widely, as if just waking up, Sonny entered the kitchen with a teacup and a cookie in her hand. She seemed to be unharmed, but she stopped walking when she noticed Jack holding the vial.

"I see you're awake, but what did you plan on doing with that?" she asked, making her way to his bedside. "Play catch? How do you know that wouldn't blow us both up?"

Both surprised and relieved to see her, he had momentarily forgotten he was even holding the vial. "I couldn't find my flashlight. But how are you awake?" Jack asked, dropping the vial back into the drawer. "Are we still in the Valentine's Day spirit's villa?"

The music from the piano stopped short as a tall man who had dark, curly hair and wore a white lab coat entered the kitchen with a plate of fruit and sandwiches. His expression was hidden under a dramatic white mask that hovered just in front of his face. However, the mask appeared to be smiling slightly. As the man turned, the masked turned as well, making it impossible to see his actual face. Jack felt the slightest amount of jealousy and dislike but didn't understand why.

"Actually, that vial is filled with a warming medication made from a rare species of plant that blooms only during spring and only during months that have two full moons," the man said from behind the muffling mask as he offered Jack the plate. "Would you care for something to eat?"

Jack reluctantly took a sandwich, not knowing if this man could be trusted or not. Because of the mask, he couldn't even tell if the doctor was looking at him or in another direction, but he thought it better not to ask about it. For some reason, the closer the masked man came to him, the more uneasy Jack felt. He took an immediate dislike to the man. In any case, he was confident that if he didn't ask about the concealment, Sonny's curiosity would eventually win out if she hadn't already taken notes on the subject.

After an approving nod from her, Jack began eating. Noticing how hungry he was, he remembered they had both recently eaten lunch. This brought up a few new questions. "How long have I been out?" Jack asked woozily, getting off the table. "Why are we in the kitchen? And where exactly is my flashlight?"

"Oh yes, forgive my rudeness," the masked man said, placing the plate on the counter. "I'm Dr. Maurice de Luca."

"He is the Spirit of Valentine's Day and a botanist," Sonny stated, looking at him a bit dreamily. "That's why he keeps so many rare plants."

"Yes, but I do dabble in medicine, chemistry, and psychology as well," said Maurice. "I used cross-pollination to create an antidote for the amount of dream dust your friend had inhaled. She recovered yesterday, but I had to treat the wounds on her hands and make sure they did not become infected. You appeared to have a fair amount of the same substance on your fingers as well. Unfortunately, I don't exactly have a medical facility here at the hotel, so I had to use the kitchen."

Jack blinked twice and held his head. "Did you say she woke up yesterday?" he asked the doctor. "How long have I been out?"

"Over twenty-four hours," stated Maurice. "That's how long the serum takes to remove all of the petrification. You should recover just fine, however. No broken bones or serious injuries."

Relieved his organs hadn't been harvested, Jack finished his sandwich. Now he was more worried about the time they had left before midnight. "And my flashlight?" he asked.

"I would assume it would still be outside in the courtyard if you dropped it," stated the doctor as he checked Jack's vitals. "When I heard the statues moving outside, I knew someone must have triggered an alarm. I ordered a halt to the system after I noticed you had been stung by a rose thorn. You should count yourself lucky."

Jack found it difficult to see how this was true. "Lucky? I've been unconscious for a day." He was visibly frustrated.

"Well, you see, the roses have different attributes, and the closer you get to the house, the more hazardous the thorns are." The doctor detached Jack's monitors. The thorns that struck you paralyzed you, so I had to give you a simple injection. Some of the other thorns are quicker when it comes to death. Still, it was lucky you made it in before it stopped your brain function, or you'd be in a coma. But that does bring a question of my own to mind." Placing the plate on the counter, he turned, and his mask seemed as if its eyebrow had risen slightly. "How exactly did you get inside my villa?"

Jack eyed his skeleton key card, wondering if this spirit could be trusted. Sonny, however, seemed almost too eager to answer.

"Jack has a skeleton key card because he's the owner's son," she said brightly.

Glaring at Sonny, Jack lifted himself off the gurney completely. "I asked room service what to do when she wouldn't wake up, and they sent me here. I tried knocking, but there was no answer." Jack waited before continuing, believing the spirit would be angry he had broken into his villa. More than anything, he was hoping his heart would not be the next to set atop the cupboard. After all, Sonny was already acting unusually, and he felt more distaste for the spirit as time went on.

Maurice directed them to accompany him to his white room and walked through the kitchen door as they followed. The moment they entered, Jack noted the door leading outside in case they needed a quick exit. The room was pure white, similar to the blank room on the first floor, except for small statues of babies with wings and arrows standing with one foot touching a pedestal positioned in each corner. A white grand piano was placed in the center with an easel and paints beside it. A white sofa faced them. At first, Jack thought it odd to paint in a room with so much white, but he quickly remembered that everything in the hotel was odd. They sat on the sofa as Maurice sat on the piano bench across from them.

"Well, I suppose I can't blame you for barging in," Maurice said as he played a classical piece on the piano. "I can understand your urgency for your friend. I must not have heard you when I was playing and painting, but it was very dangerous to come here without prior warning." As he got up from the bench, the piano continued playing without interruption. Standing at the easel, he continued his portrait of what looked like a city that had actual sparkling lights. "But I do wonder why you did not turn off the security alarm first?"

Looking at Sonny, who had been watching Maurice paint, Jack attempted to think back to his entrance inside but couldn't remember much before the statues had attacked him. "What security alarm?" he asked blankly.

Holding the paintbrush up with a bit of blue on the tip, the doctor pointed at Jack's key card. "The statues and rose bushes are all part of the hotel security defense for my villa.

There's a slot on the inside, next to the door, that turns it off. You could have simply used your card. The manager insisted all of the holidays and symbols be well secured because of Phoenix's, and now the April Fool's spirit's, disappearance. I truly believe it's unneeded for me, however. I've been alone for quite some time, and my abilities are quite strong on their own, but I prefer to avoid confrontation unless necessary."

A small wave of jealousy overwhelmed Jack as he blurted out, "I always thought Valentine's Day was just made up by the greeting card companies. How powerful could you honestly be?"

Sonny gave Jack an incredibly cold glare that reminded him of his mother, as if she couldn't believe his rudeness. The doctor, however, waived his paint brush. "Oh, no, no, no," he said as he continued painting. "There's a long history to Saint Valentine's Day. In much earlier years, the laws proclaimed by the king prohibited women to marry any soldiers in Rome, believing, without families, they would have no distractions. The ruler at the time believed this would create much stronger warriors. That is why my statues are formed after Roman soldiers. A Roman priest decided to perform secret marriages against the law, until he was imprisoned. There, he performed a miracle where he healed the blind child of the jailer that kept him, but that's another story. The soldiers celebrated his actions with a feast, which became the holiday my power comes from. Have you guessed what that power is?" he asked as the white mask appeared to be waiting for an answer.

Normally, Jack would try to remain reserved, but something about this spirit became increasingly unnerving to him. "I don't know, but I'm guessing it has something to do with that mask?" he said sarcastically as he rolled his eyes and tightened his fists.

"Actually, yes it does," the doctor said politely. "You may be surprised to know that these dramatic masks come from the Greek muses Thalia and Melpomene. I use it to shield myself from others, because I have the power to influence love, as well as jealousy like you are feeling now."

Taken aback, Jack began to stand up in protest until he understood that jealousy actually was the reason he resented the spirit. Sonny appeared to be coming out of the trance she was in, and her dreamy state began to vanish. She immediately grabbed for her pen and pad next to her.

"So, you cause jealousy?" Jack questioned.

The doctor shook his head. "Not exactly. My presence is able to bend those feelings, but you cannot have one without the other, which has been very dangerous in the past. Because your friend feels the positive, someone must feel an equal amount of the negative. That is the balance that wars have been created and fought for — started because of jealousy or won because of love. They are very powerful emotions, but that's more of a secondary power of holiday spirits. Your father has come for guidance a few times, actually, because of your mother . . . and for you."

"You've met my father?" Jack asked earnestly. "When did you see him last? That's not his heart in the kitchen, is it?"

Sonny's head shot up from her pad, and she looked from Jack to the doctor. "Of course not," Maurice replied sternly as his masked followed. "The heart in my kitchen is a therapeutic tool, but, no, it's not his. From what he has described to me, it's not difficult to tell you are his son. I haven't had a visit from him in over a week, sadly. It does become lonely here. However, I must not elaborate. After all, he is a patient."

A clock on the wall behind him that Jack hadn't noticed before chimed loudly as it struck six o'clock. Jack leaped out of his seat, almost knocking the mask off Maurice as he remembered they were under time restraints.

"Well, I appreciate you helping Sonny and me, but we really have to hurry," Jack said, making his way to the door.

Sonny stood up, still blushing slightly, and joined him at the front door. "What about the plan?" she asked quietly. "How are we supposed to know what holiday happened last, or did you find out already?"

"No, but maybe we should discuss that when we leave." Jack hoped she wouldn't continue talking about it in front of the spirit.

Jack became nervous as the doctor made his way over to the phone and spoke to room service. After a moment, he asked for the villa in room thirteen on the twentieth floor.

"Hello, Mother," he said brightly, turning away from Jack and Sonny and removing his mask. Sonny felt a strong flutter as if she were being hypnotized. "Yes, I have a small favor to ask of your brilliant talents. I'm rehearsing a small play about a hotel mystery and was wondering if you could make two attendant uniforms with universal fittings. . . . Yes just like those. . . . Oh, you are always so kind to me. Thank you, Mother."

Neither Jack nor Sonny understood what he was doing. The doctor hung up the phone and repositioned the mask over his face as he made his way to the door. "Your father advised me just a few months ago about a reading he had in the city," he said thoughtfully. "He told me you would need my assistance, and I assumed when you arrived that he meant medically. But now, I realize I was partly mistaken."

"My father had a reading done?" Jack asked, remembering what the fortune teller Luminista had told him about being sent to wait at the hotel until he arrived. "He must have been the one who sent for me in the first place. He had a reading done and sent Luminista to do one for me. But why?"

"I don't understand," Sonny said with a confused look. "What exactly are the uniforms for?"

Maurice opened the door of his home and escorted them to the villa's entrance. The roses had returned to their original size, and the statues were once again unmoving on their pedestals. If they hadn't attacked Jack, he would say the garden was pretty and enchanting. However, since they had attacked him, he now thought it would be fun to use the garden as a track for bulldozer practice. The sun shone brightly as they walked along the path of the majestic courtyard. Passing by the smashed mound of dirt where he had collapsed, Jack searched the ground until he spotted his flashlight's handle reflecting the light from above. Vines wriggled away as he picked it up. He noticed three tiny sun-shaped balls floating in the magnifying glass. As much as he tried to wipe them off, they lingered, continuing to float around inside the glass as if it had somehow soaked in the sun's rays. Satisfied that he had found it in one piece, Jack placed the flashlight into his pocket and continued following the doctor.

When they arrived at the villa entrance, they found a package wrapped in plain brown paper and tied with twine sitting in front of the door. Maurice opened the package containing two attendant uniforms along with hats and shoes and handed them to Jack. "There you go. Mother may have her faults, but she really is an excellent tailor," said the doctor. He watched as Sonny and Jack exchanged looks of confusion. Jack tried his best to not drop anything as the mention of the word "tailor" made him think back to Luminista.

"Thank you very much, doctor," Sonny said gratefully, "but what do we need attendant uniforms for?"

"Well, you need to find holiday spirits who are staying here, correct?" replied Maurice, "And besides the manager, the only ones who have access to a list of guests would be—"

"The attendants," Jack finished. "When Emanuel checked us in, he had a list of guests. They must have it somewhere in the back office, and we can narrow down the holiday spirits."

Sonny nodded in agreement. "It would be the perfect plan to go unnoticed."

As they thanked the doctor, the hovering drama mask revealed a small triumphant smile. Maurice opened the door to the villa. "Now, you two should hurry along. I'm sure my plants in the city are very thirsty, so the sooner we can all leave the hotel, the better. Oh, and, before I forget, there's one more thing." He removed two heart-shaped chocolates wrapped in red plastic from his lab coat pocket and handed them to Sonny. "Just in case you begin to feel ill again, take two of these and call me in the morning."

# Chapter 8
## Gifted

The day seemed to go by faster than Jack could keep up. The sun seemed to be diving down into the horizon as night quickly approached, and he wasn't sure how much closer he was to finding the New Year's spirit, the Infinite Hourglass, or his father before midnight. Using the area between the villa door and the hazy wall, they changed into their newly acquired attendant uniforms. As he pulled the loosely fitting pants over his jeans, they shortened and became the perfect size and length. The jacket, shoes, and even hat seemed to adjust as soon as he had held them in his hands long enough.

As they dressed, Jack explained to Sonny what had happened when he left and returned to discover her asleep in bed. He told her about finding his room destroyed, being attacked by the warrior statues, and ducking the garden thorns. As usual, she took notes, asking for the occasional detail, but didn't seem too surprised that someone had broken into his room.

"It seems quite obvious that whoever took Phoenix and the April Fool would try to stop us from searching," Sonny said, tying her shoe laces. "But why destroy your room?"

Jack had read a chapter about this in his clues book before. "If they were after me, whoever it was would have left as soon as they realized I wasn't there. So, they were definitely looking for something, but what would I have that someone would want?" He thought about his flashlight and then the button he'd found.

He placed his attendant hat atop his head, adjusting the brim to hide his face as well as he could. "There are fifty-two attendants working here, including the manager. And Emanuel said he knew them all, so we should avoid him as much as possible."

Sonny buttoned the last few gold buttons of the red jacket. "How do I look?" She stood at attention. "Believable?"

Jack glanced at her and gave her a thumbs-up as he concentrated on the discarded packaging the disguises had been wrapped in. A note addressed to Dr. de Luca was sticking out from beneath the twine:

> *I tailored this one to match the other exactly. I hope*
> *it is too your liking,*
> *Your Favorite Mother*

"What 'other one' do you think she means?" Sonny asked, reading over Jack's shoulder.

"I think she means another uniform," Jack stated, wondering if Sonny was now thinking the same thing he was.

"I know this doesn't look very flattering, but Maurice helped us get these uniforms when he did not have to," Sonny defended. "I'm sure he would have tossed the note if he had anything to do with the missing holidays or any of this at all."

Jack thought about it and, for the moment, decided she was right. There was no clear motive, and his actions didn't seem at all hostile. Besides, if the doctor was a friend of his father's, he wanted to be able to trust him. "We shouldn't make any conclusions or rule anyone out until we find out who all the suspects are," he said, finishing the placement of his disguise. "We should head to the attendants' area before it gets any later. It's almost dark, and we're running out of time."

Taking the televator down to the fifty-second floor, their fears increased drastically. The blue light of the keys made them anxious, and although Sonny was optimistic, Jack feared they would be easily spotted by someone. They found the hall fairly crowded with guests who were lined up for dinner. Luckily, the manager's desk was empty, but attendants were still rushing around busily. It seemed the only one they would have to get past was Number Fifty-Two. He stood at the door, directing guests, as usual. But he appeared nervous as he frequently checked the east and west halls.

Jack and Sonny hurried past the fountain with flowing colors of orange, purple, and blue mimicking the setting of the sun. Passing the managers desk and the line of guest at the lounge, they rushed to the right but were stopped by the attendant.

"I'm sorry, but who are you two?" he asked politely.

They froze, turning around hesitantly. Jack kept his brim low as Sonny started to speak when Thomas interrupted her.

"I'm sorry. I'm still pretty new. It's hard to remember so many names in the same uniform. I was just wondering if there were any new orders since it's getting closer to nightfall or what news we may have about the missing holidays."

Sonny did her best to change her voice. "Nothing yet. Manny . . . I mean Number One hasn't told you anything new, has he?"

Number Fifty-Two looked at her curiously but shrugged it off. "Not since they found information that puts Mr. Shadow on the first floor when the New Year's spirit went missing. Quite a few believe the rumors are true about Father inventing Mr. Shadow's symbols to create a new dark holiday twelve years ago. We still haven't had word from the owner yet. Rumor is he's gone missing, too. Oh, excuse me." He left to attend to a few guests who were asking for directions to The Candy Garden. Jack and Sonny exchanged looks, but Jack was determined to get the guest list before officially suspecting anyone else.

He followed Sonny down the west hall as she went through her notepad for directions. They walked by dozens of doors before reaching the very last one at the end of the hall with a swinging door labeled Attendants' Quarters. Before he had a chance to come up with any sort of story in case they ran into another employee, Sonny had already pushed the door open and walked in.

The room wasn't very large compared to the villas, but it was about four times bigger than the regular hotel rooms. There were tables, chairs, a refrigerator, a television, a few plants, and a small kitchen area. Another door on the opposite wall read Attendants' Bedrooms, where Jack assumed they slept when not needed. They found themselves lucky, because only one attendant seemed to be inside. He was shorter than the others, maybe an inch shorter than Sonny, and he was reading a book titled *Doomsday Approaching: How to Build a Panic Room*. He only glanced up for a moment when they entered and then continued reading.

Trying not to be suspicious, they walked behind him and sat at the last table toward the back of the room. "We should try to find a desk or filing cabinet, or something that would have papers in it," Jack whispered to Sonny.

"How do you know it's not at the manager's desk?" she asked. "Isn't that where Manny checked us in?"

Jack tried to remain as quiet as possible. "He did, but when we were leaving, he gave the sign-in sheet to Number Forty-Three, who came this way with it remember? This is the only logical place it could be."

Searching by the refrigerator, Sonny looked through instructional papers, hotel pamphlets, and attendant sign-up sheets. Jack tried his best not to disrupt the other attendant as he went from table to table, but neither of them found anything. The other attendant hadn't seemed to notice. He continued staring into his book without a glance in their direction.

Several minutes passed before Jack had finished searching among the counters. He shrugged at Sonny, who seemed to be eyeing the attendant suspiciously. She pointed discreetly at the table where the attendant was still sitting. Beneath his elbow lay a small stack of papers with a list on top. Sonny had apparently noticed their names; she and Jack were the last guests to sign in.

"How do we get it?" Jack mouthed silently. The attendant still hadn't looked up, and Jack began to think he may have fallen asleep while reading. As usual, Sonny had brought out her notepad, but after writing only one word, she handed it to Jack and sat down boldly in a chair beside the attendant.

"That looks interesting," she said to the attendant as he read. "Have you always been interested in these panic rooms?"

Jack wasn't sure how bringing attention to herself would help them until he read the word *copy* written on the pad. At once, he understood what to do. However, it became increasingly difficult because the attendant refused to provide more to Sonny's questions than a head nod or a shoulder shrug. His elbow remained firmly on the guest list, and Jack quickly began to doubt this plan of hers until the door burst open and an exasperated Number Fifty-Two stood in the doorway.

"We need all the attendants to the lobby immediately. Number One is making an announcement . . . sir," he added.

It wasn't until the attendant stood up to follow Number Fifty-Two that they realized his badge number had the number two embroidered onto it. As the other attendant reluctantly followed Number Fifty-Two, Jack quickly set the list on top of the notepad and clicked the pen to copy the guest list. Then he rushed behind Sonny as the group exited.

As they walked back to the main lobby, they examined the list. They discovered that each spirit's villa and floor had been written next to each of the signatures, making it easier to figure out who was staying on each floor. However, the spirits of the most recent holidays weren't currently guests at the hotel. From the forty-fourth floor to the fifty-second, there was only one floor with a holiday villa being used.

"We should be checking floors corresponding with holidays that would happen close to New Year's Eve, but I only see one spirit's villa on a floor that's even close," Jack whispered to Sonny.

Taking the notepad from Jack, Sonny flipped to a page to ask for directions to the villa. "When we get to the lobby, we should be able to get lost in the crowd fairly easily," she responded.

As they followed the attendants into the lobby, they noticed that the others had already arrived. Red-and-gold uniforms formed a large semi-circle surrounding Emanuel like loyal subjects to a king. Sonny made sure she and Jack stayed in the back of the group for easy escape as the manager made his announcement.

"As we grow closer to the final hours of the year, we also grow closer to uncertainty. But we still should not give up," the manager said with a slight smile. "Although the whereabouts of the hourglass, the owner, and the missing holiday spirits are unknown, I feel strongly that we have narrowed down the possibilities of where they could be. It is now imperative that guests stay in their assigned rooms until further notice, so we may conclude our investigation." Number One began handing out a sheet to each attendant. Sonny pulled Jack toward the east hall, believing it would be the best time to exit unnoticed.

"The holiday is on this floor, so it shouldn't be too hard to get there," Jack whispered, moving farther away from the attendants. "He's the only spirit staying here whose holiday is the closest to when the days began repeating, and he's our best chance to find out what happened leading up to it."

"What makes you think the spirit is a man?" She pointed to the name on the list. "States here the spirit's name is Holly, you know?"

"Well, I assumed with the holiday symbol being—" he began as Sonny started to snicker. "What's so funny?"

"I thought you didn't believe in him?" Sonny giggled as Jack rolled his eyes.

Using the map on her notepad, they found a wall with a large wreath placed upon it where the villa door should be. It was extremely cold, like a walk-in freezer, and frost lined the edges of the doors. Jack was able to see every warm breath he made in the cold leave his lips like steam from a boiling pot. He was glad he had an extra layer of clothing on as he thought back to the fortune teller Luminista. Her room was near, but he noticed that its door handle was still missing. He removed his flashlight from his pocket. The three tiny suns still stuck in the glass as he shined the flashlight through the wall. The light gleamed onto a new stand-alone door decorated in pine-green. It had one slanted red stripe and a small key card slot. As they stepped through the wall, snow fluttered from above, instantly covering the ground. The beam from a single star above the door allowed them to easily find the slot.

"Once we get in, don't forget what Maurice said about the hotel security," Sonny said softly. "There should be a scanner near the door for the skeleton key card to disable it."

"Right," he agreed, remembering the giant statues and rose bushes. "Worst game of dodge ball I've ever played."

As he slid his key card into the slot, Jack heard sleigh bells ring when the door unlocked. Walking through the doorway, they stepped onto a welcome mat in a small hilly field covered in a thick blanket of snow. The villa strongly reminded Jack of the snow globes from the rest stop. Rays from the sun glistened on icicles, creating a faint rainbow in front of them. To the far left was a frozen pond, where much shorter people appeared to be ice skating. Beyond the field was a small village of several wooden cabins encircling two bigger cabins with pine trees scattered around them. The two cabins in the center were easily twice as large as the others, and white smoke billowed from the one on the left. Gravel roads intertwined with each other throughout the village until they were cut off by the hills.

Before they could take a step farther inside, an alarm sounded and the tiny people who were ice skating ran behind a hill. Two giant igloos rose above the hills from the ground a few hundred yards in front of them. A dozen snowmen with carrot noses exited one by one and towered over the trees. The ground trembled violently, knocking the snow off cabins and trees as they marched in unison toward Sonny and Jack. Their burning-red eyes heated the area around their eye sockets just enough to show a partially metal skull. It wasn't long before Jack realized these snowmen were actually machines.

Snowballs the size of boulders whizzed by Sonny as they were shot from cannons built into the chests of the snow army. Jack stood stunned at the winter wonderland dream that had suddenly become a nightmare until Sonny pulled him down.

"Jack!" she yelled, searching the edges of the door. "I could use some help turning off the alarm. I don't see the slot! Find the slot!" Rushing to help her, Jack was able to duck snowballs. The snowballs struck everywhere they had been standing, freezing the spots instantly. Toy soldiers began marching out next, launching red sacks that instantly grappled anything they landed on.

"I don't see any key slots!" Jack yelled as Sonny tilted her head and stared at his feet. "What is it?" he asked, looking around while ducking a sack.

She quickly pushed him off the welcome mat and lifted it up to reveal a hidden slot. Jack fumbled through his many pockets for his key card. The snowmen's eyes grew brighter red, and they began swarming in. Jack scrambled to push the key card into the lock. Just as the heat around the snowmen's eyes had melted much of the snow from their sockets, they powered down and stood motionless at the bottom of the hill like giant toys with dead batteries

"A welcome mat?" Jack sighed in relief. "Should've been obvious."

"Seemed very out of place," Sonny said, falling back into the snow. She began waving her arms and legs back and forth, making a snow angel.

A man in a full military fatigue uniform of red, black, and white walked up to them. He was wearing black boots and dark sunglasses. He carried what appeared to be an empty red sack as if to drag them off with it. It was easy to tell that he had recently lost a lot of weight. His skin was sagging on his face beneath his white beard. His nose along with his cheeks was red. He seemed almost frail, but he had a strong demeanor about him, like he was not willing to quit. He was accompanied by two much shorter ice skaters, who could barely be seen behind him, marching in the same fashion and wearing fatigues as well. As he approached Jack, who was breathing hard in the cold air, he snapped his fingers, and the two shorter people vanished then reappeared behind Sonny and Jack.

"How did you get in and disable the security?" the tall man asked with a gruff voice. "Whoever it was that sent you should know that we will not let her go without a fight!"

Before either of them could answer, a shadow peered over the hill, blocking the sun shining in Sonny's face. As she and Jack looked up, a hooded figure glared back at them without making a sound. Jack believed it was Mr. Shadow, but the figure was wearing a red cloak and was at least nine feet tall. However, the voice surprised him more than anything.

"Come now, Clause. They're only children," the hooded figure said in a very pleasant voice. Her voice sounded so sweet that Jack could have sworn she was singing. "Invite them inside. I'm sure they must be cold."

"Clause?" Sonny questioned the man's attire and frail body. "Surely you don't mean Santa Clause?"

The man chuckled, "We should get you inside as she has requested. Follow, please."

Sonny and Jack followed as the red-hooded figure along with Clause led the way. The two small people followed behind them. They walked along the snowy path toward the larger of the middle cabins. The sun shone brightly on them all as they walked silently, but it was still freezing. The snow glistened from the trees, showing no signs of melting.

When they entered the large cabin on the right, they immediately felt warm. The embers of a fireplace popped loudly and radiated heat. Wreaths hung high above on each section of the wall all around with a floating candle between each one. It all seemed to be arranged around a single giant

Christmas tree at the very end of the room. What looked to be a small toy polar bear sat in front, as if it were a gift for someone. He had never seen a decorated tree so big. It was easily twice as tall as the woman in red, but the star floating on top really made Jack curious. As it became blindingly bright but then began to flicker and dull, he knew that it, unlike other Christmas tree stars, was an actual star. Despite all this, there still seemed to be a cheeriness missing from the villa.

"That's part of the North Star," the tall woman said, removing her hood. "It allows Santa to increase his abilities to deliver." Her long blond hair flowed down, curving perfectly around her rosy cheeks and emerald-green eyes and down her back. She was truly stunning, and she beamed a beautiful smile.

Instantly, Jack felt as if he were falling back into time to the first Christmas he could remember; both of his parents were smiling down at him as he unwrapped the blue-and-white packaging to reveal the detective's kit. He knew Sonny was going through a similar flashback as a tear rolled down her cheek and she smiled.

"Are you Holly?" Sonny asked timidly, for a change. "The Spirit of Christmas?"

"Well, you didn't think she was Mrs. Clause, did ya?" Clause said, waving the little people ahead; they scurried forward. With a snap of their fingers, they produced wooden rocking chairs for them all to sit on.

"So, you are Santa?" Sonny asked in awe.

"No, he is Clause, and I am Holly," said the woman as she dismissed the shorter people with a short bow to them both. "These are two of our many helpers for the holiday."

Jack watched as the helpers left the room. "Wait, are they supposed to be elves?"

Clause chuckled at this, too, as he sat down in his rocking chair and removed his glasses. "Well, I guess that's what you dreamers have been calling them for centuries now. They are not much different from any of us really, including you. They just live about five times longer. They've been helping us for at least a dozen decades now."

The toy polar bear began to gnaw on the toy fish in the corner, and Jack realized it wasn't a toy, but a real baby polar bear. When Holly followed his eyes to the cub, she giggled, and the polar bear dissolved into snowflakes. It reappeared in her lap as she sat down in a particularly large chair and patted its head. It had pure-white fur and ice-blue eyes like glaciers with snowflakes for pupils.

"A gift from Old Man Winter." Holly smiled. "One of my favorite companions," she said sweetly. Clause made a noise by clearing his throat. "Along with you, of course, Clause." Clause smiled slightly at this and nodded affirmatively.

It was quiet for a moment as the fire crackled in the background. Sonny repositioned herself in her seat, sitting up straight, and glared at Clause. "Excuse me, sir, but you look nothing like my grandfather."

It was hard to distinguish from the beady eyes and sunken cheeks whether he was angry or amused at this. "Why do you think I should look like your grandfather?" Clause asked seriously, returning the glare.

Sonny hadn't faltered at all at his look and continued to speak as if she had simply asked about the weather. "Well, my grandfather was an avid Christmas enthusiast," she said politely, "And when he dressed as Santa Clause, he had a large belly, rosy cheeks, and a full white beard and was jolly." Jack feared what she might say next, and he hoped she'd choose her words wisely but knew that was not in her nature. "But you seem . . . grumpy."

The flames from the fireplace danced in Clause's eyes, and he looked ready to unleash something dreadful from his bag as he reached for it. Placing his entire arm up to the shoulder deep inside the bag, he pulled out a tray with two piping-hot cups of tea. Jack hesitantly took the cup offered to him. Sonny followed suit, getting comfortable as if preparing to be tucked into bed and read a bedtime story.

"Mmmm," she said excitedly after sipping, "Tastes just like candy canes."

Normally, Jack wasn't much of a tea drinker, but trying his best to not be rude, he took a sip and was immediately surprised. "Sugar cookies?" he said in awe and drank more.

Clause grinned. "I'm sure you've heard many stories of Santa Clause and the origins." He glanced at Holly, who continued to pet her polar bear. "But the truth is, as one of the first few symbols created by the Spirit of Father's Day, I came from part of the personality of the Spirit of Christmas as an early model, or *prototype*, you could say. My original purpose was to be a woodsman and aid her in building the Christmas Village. However, as the holiday itself changed, the need for a different symbol came, as well. I was divided to protect the spirit as Santa was created to judge the children and reward accordingly. He was born from her kindness, and as I was born from her loyalty and strength, I soon became one of her loyal protectors. He aids her in spreading the message of the holiday by giving to others, and that's when the stories began. Some partly true, others somewhat stretched."

He chuckled a booming, "Ho, Ho, Ho!" It shook the entire cabin, causing a bit of snow to fall from the roof. He quickly cleared his throat and continued. "We are actually identical, normally, but it must be obvious why I don't look my usual self and may seem . . . 'grumpy' as you put it."

Considering his frail condition, Jack made an educated guess. "Because Christmas never came?" Clause nodded in agreement. Jack couldn't help but wonder if these could be the twin symbols Father had discussed. He couldn't, however, imagine any of them being responsible for a dark holiday.

"Without fulfilling his purpose, he will wither away as if starving," Holly said softly with sympathetic eyes.

"You must have some idea of who has the hourglass?" Sonny asked, ready to write on her pad. "Or Mr. Phoenix?"

"Or my father?" Jack finished.

A sudden knock on the door startled Sonny, causing her to drop her pad. Clause stood from his chair, and after answering the door, brought in two gift-wrapped packages — a red one with silver bow and a green one with a gold bow. After handing them both to Holly, he excused himself and left the three of them alone in the cabin.

"There isn't much I can tell you that you have not discovered yourselves," she said as the baby polar bear vanished into snowflakes. "I'm sure you've attempted to find information on a similar event that occurred many years ago and found nothing. And as holiday spirits, we are all forbidden by the elders from speaking on the matter. However, there are ways around that if you have the ability."

Both Jack and Sonny stood as she extended a gift to each of them. "To you, Jack, I give a physical gift. Because of the amount of time left in the day, I would suggest opening it the moment you have left the villa," Holly said rather seriously but still with warmth. "However, your gift, Sonny, is one as strong as your imagination and should be used only when the moment is right. I should hope you both remember how important it is to give as well as to receive."

As the spirit escorted them out of the cabin, they noticed Clause and the two smaller people preparing what looked to be a four-wheel drive military vehicle that matched his red-camouflage uniform. He nodded to Sonny and Jack as they went up the snowy hill and to the front door. Holly placed her hood back on, and the Christmas cheer began to fade from Jack and Sonny.

"I wish you both a blessed evening," she said from beneath the hood. Her body began to glow like the North Star until they were forced to look away. In an instant, the light dimmed and she was gone.

Using the flashlight, Jack found their way back through the wall and into the cold east hallway, where they were unexpectedly stopped by someone.

"Where did you two just come from?" Number One questioned.

"Um . . . ," Jack stammered, trying to hide his face with his hat. "We were . . . "

"We were just picking these packages up for delivery from a guest," Sonny said quickly.

Number One appeared more disheveled than before and looked upon them with much uncertainty. "You would do well to hurry yourselves now that our newest suspects are the two dreamers along with the Spirit of Father's Day."

"The dreamers?" Jack asked, taken aback. "How's that possible?"

"Were you both too busy to be involved at the meeting that happened not moments ago to hear they were the last ones to be seen with Father?" asked the manager sarcastically. "Or was the history lesson U.S. showed today about him not to your liking?"

"Oh, no. It just must have slipped his mind," Sonny recovered. "We've just been so busy. We will definitely hurry and get these delivered at once, sir." Leaving Number One standing and looking quizzically after them, they hurried to the televators and went directly to their floor.

"Do you really think it's smart to go back to our rooms now that we're suspected?" Sonny asked as they left the televator.

"As long as we have the uniforms on, we should be alright," replied Jack as he placed the skeleton key into his door slot and continued inside. "If Emanuel didn't recognize us, we should be able to hide here and explain we were searching if anyone asks." He led them inside only to see that the room was once again immaculate. Everything had been replaced, cleaned, and tidied up as if the destruction that had happened earlier had never existed.

"Housekeeping possibly?" Sonny asked, but Jack decided there were more important things to worry about. He shut the door behind them hastily.

They avoided sitting on the bed for fear of falling asleep immediately. Jack paced as he spoke. "Okay, so now everyone's after us along with Father," Jack said exasperatedly. "And it has something to do with the past events they discussed at the meeting. Emanuel said something about U.S. giving them a history lesson. We can't exactly ask anyone, or they might find out we're not really attendants. So what do we do now? If none of the holidays can tell us, then how do we find out with less than five hours before midnight?"

"What about the gift Holly gave you?" Sonny said, pointing at the wrapped package Jack had clearly forgotten. "She said specifically to open it when we left the villa. Maybe it will have some use."

Jack sat in the desk chair and began prying the wrappings from the present. As the gold bow and green paper hit the floor, he opened the box, exposing two Blueberry Fiz bottles with a note attached that read: *To your good health and good wisdom. Merry Christmas.*

After reading the note, Jack looked to Sonny for some sort of explanation, but she seemed as clueless as he did. He handed a bottle to her and opened one for himself.

"Well, the other Fiz drinks had special effects, like energy for the island cream, and the brightberry helped me remember things. Maybe this one will too?" Jack said.

After examining it briefly, he brought the bottle to his lips and drank. The taste of blueberries, pomegranate, and carbonated vanilla cream rushed over his tongue. After watching for a moment to see if he felt any differently, Sonny began to follow his lead and drank.

"We have to go now!" Jack exclaimed as he leaped from his chair.

"Why? Where are we going?" she asked, lowering her bottle. "Do you have an idea?"

"Bring your gift with you," Jack replied, opening the door to leave. "I think I know where we can go to see exactly what happened twelve years ago. Come on, we have a movie to catch."

# Chapter 9
## The Dark Holiday

"I still don't understand why we're going to the forty-fourth floor." Sonny caught up to Jack in the televator.

Jack was busy muttering to himself as his mind raced with possibilities. Sonny had trouble getting his attention until the doors opened, revealing a new hallway. It was much more arid than the floor they were staying on, like dry summer heat after a streak of days without rainfall. Seven doors lined the wall and streamers in red, white, and blue hung over the doorways. Fireworks went off intermittently, and the smell of salt water and beach sand clung to the air.

"It's quite patriotic, isn't it?" Sonny stated, breaking Jack out of his trance.

He removed his flashlight and began walking along the bare wall, pointing his light at it. He didn't begin talking to Sonny again until he found a stand-alone door and escorted Sonny through the wall.

"I'm not exactly sure what else may be behind this door," Jack whispered carefully. He appeared to still be thinking of possible scenarios, but the Blueberry Fiz had already begun to wear off. "I'll explain everything when we get in."

He stared at the handle to the door, which had been inspired by the United States flag. The closer Jack moved to it, the more it appeared to be waving as if on a pole in the wind. After placing the key card into the slot, he waited for it to open. But it remained locked. He shrugged at Sonny, who still wasn't sure why they had come there at all. After watching Jack try twice more with the card, Sonny couldn't help but stare at the door as it continued to wave.

"Maybe the card's been blocked?" Jack said, hanging his head.

Sonny continued watching the flag as its waving began to slow. "Look." She pointed as Jack raised his head and the flag began waving normally again.

"What? Did it open?" He attempted to push it open, but it remained just as immovable. "It's still not open."

Stepping closer to the door, Sonny tilted her head down slightly, watching the flag's movement slow once again. Then, as she removed her hat completely, the flag only moved at half the speed. "You should try your card again, and possibly remember to remove your hat in front of the flag this time?" Sonny smirked. After he had placed his hat under his arm, the flag stopped all movement. Jack tried his card once more, and it unlocked, allowing them inside.

"It must be a test of patriotism or something," Jack said as they entered a dark hallway. As they walked, their steps echoed through the long hallway lined with small lights like a runway. It was quiet, and except for a small glow many yards away, they could see only the floor.

After several minutes of bewilderment about where they were going, Sonny spoke up. "I realize we're at the Independence Day spirit's villa, but I still don't understand why?"

Jack looked at her through the darkness, barely able to tell where she was. "It's really only a hunch, and it sounded smarter before we left, but I guess that was the drink." He scratched his head. "The first night we were here, I remember Emanuel telling Number Fifty-Two to finish his training video in the theater room." Although it was difficult to tell between each lit part of the floor, he saw Sonny nod for him to continue. "And earlier, when he mentioned a history lesson for the attendants from U.S. about Father, it all made sense."

They grew closer to the light at the end of the hall, which had begun to get much larger as they approached. "Alright, so we can view movies from past events, but I thought none of the holiday spirits could tell us anything?" Sonny was still baffled.

"Exactly. They can't. But after seeing Holly, I'm hoping that means whatever happened twelve years ago with the dark holiday, we will be able to see for ourselves instead of hearing it from a holiday spirit." They had stopped at a wooden podium without realizing it. An enormous screen larger than Jack had ever seen displayed a white canvas off to the right corner as an older gentleman walked up to them quietly. He stopped short of the podium, searching his pockets and then pulling out a pair of thick black glasses. He put them on and smiled.

"Welcome to the theater," he said gingerly in a gruff voice. "What may I help you two view today? We have a lovely romantic comedy from the 1970s and horror films from a quite a few periods."

He wasn't at all what Jack had imagined. His clothes matched those of a movie theater attendant down to the flashlight and black bow tie. Only his beard and wrinkled face resembled the symbol Jack had expected. "Are you U.S.?" Jack asked. "Uncle Sam?"

"No, not today," the theater attendant replied brightly. "I'm Usher Sam. I attend to the viewing of history's monumental events in the theater room. Uncle Sam's availability is strictly on July Fourth. The Spirit of Independence Day has many individuals to assist him. Now, what can I show you today?"

Sonny stared at the glow reflecting from the movie screen onto his smiling face. She could see how eager the usher was to help. "Well, we were wondering what you could show us of the dark holiday twelve years ago."

The usher's smile faltered a bit as two tickets popped up from the podium before he answered. "The holiday spirits were banned from speaking about it once the judgment was made, but as I am not a holiday spirit, we do have it available to view." Reaching beneath the podium, he pulled out two pairs of 3-D glasses with black-and-white lenses. "I can only show events that happened here in the United States. Lucky for you, the dark holiday was almost finished in New York. Follow me, please."

The usher escorted them up the stairs to the seats in front of the large movie screen. Jack was surprised to see there were only enough seats for eight people in the entire theater. Two were stationed each row. Jack and Sonny sat in the last two seats as the usher climbed the steps behind them into a booth, casting a shadow against the screen as he worked. "You may want to put on your glasses now," Sam shouted down to them. Jack heard him ruffling through metal tins and fiddling with the projector until, a few moments later, the reel began to play and the room grew darker.

Jack and Sonny placed the glasses onto their faces, staring through the gray combination of colors. However, the moment the rims touched their faces, the glasses snapped into place, becoming affixed to their ears and eyes. As much as they scratched at the eyepieces and rubbed their faces, the glasses stayed permanently affixed.

A solid image of a young, brown-haired woman wearing a black silk dress laced with orange became clear on the movie screen. The screen had stopped just before she began pacing in an empty corridor of a stone building. The candy decorations at the bottom of her dress were in mid-swish onscreen.

Attempting to get the usher's attention or to call for help, Jack began pushing down on the armrests to get out of his seat, but he made no progress. He seemed to be glued into his seat, tethered there by invisible ties. Before he could register what to do, Sonny nudged him with a panicked expression Jack hadn't seen from her before. The sound of gears powering up was followed by a glow around the edges of the movie screen as it began to move toward them slowly. And it was gaining speed. Sonny wiggled and pulled as much as she could, trying to stand up. But she stopped suddenly as the screen passed through the first set of chairs, turning them to gray stone.

"Sam, let us out of here!" Jack yelled, pulling on Sonny's arms, trying to lift her out of the seat.

The usher seemed unable to hear them over the loud reeling of the film, because he only yelled back, "What's that?"

The screen froze the second row of seats, turning them and the floor into stone, followed shortly by the third row as the screen gained speed like a locomotive. The last thing they heard before the screen ran through them was the usher advising them to hold their breaths. Sonny shut her eyes tightly, gripping the chair arm. As the screen came within inches of his face, Jack glared at the woman onscreen solidly, as if she would be the last thing he'd see.

There was a slight pause before the young woman in the black-and-orange dress began pacing again. Jack's eyes never left her, but it took a moment for him to realize that he was now in the film. He swallowed hard, hoping the bitter taste of wood and chalk would leave his mouth, as he studied the room he was now in. It may have been because everything was in black and white, but he was surprised to see that he was in a modern-day building. It was tall, like a skyscraper, with many levels of stores and shops. An amusement park ride spiraled in the center. Sonny had only now opened her eyes as the woman walked by them as if they didn't exist at all. Her dress with pieces of candy stitched into the bottom continued to swish by. She was very pretty and sweet looking, but she seemed worried as well.

A flash of light followed by black smoke drew all of their attention into a corner of the corridor as the woman went running toward it.

"Where have you been?" she asked in a sweet voice as she rushed toward the young man exiting the swirling black smoke. "I overheard a few of the holiday spirits talking about you. They found out it was your millennium prank from earlier this year. Why did you have me meet you at Times Square?"

The young man who had appeared from the smoke was wearing a shimmering, open-collared black silk shirt with orange stitching that matching the woman's dress. His baggy black pants held zippers shaped like wide jack-o'-lantern grins. His face was shaded, the way Jack would imagine a younger version of Mr. Shadow. Only his mischievous grin was visible as the man motioned the woman over to a dark area of the room.

"My dear, sweet sister, would I have you come all this way just to disappoint you?" His voice was cunning and smooth, giving Jack the same uneasy feeling he had received from Dr. de Luca. From one of the young man's many pockets, he brought out a small hourglass filled with white sand.

"How did you get that?" the young woman asked. "Where have you been?"

"Everywhere," said the young man, "I've almost fulfilled the true purpose that he's bestowed upon me. Barely challenging really, but I finally created a real holiday more powerful than any of the others."

The young woman checked over her shoulder as if she were in a hurry. "You mean Mischief Night? Did you really finish it?"

His smile became broader, like a jack-o'-lantern's. "That was only the test holiday. But, of course, I implanted it, and it took very well in Britain, Canada, and the U.S. But I've figured out how to develop a holiday that will be feared by so many, a new dark holiday using this as an artifact." He removed a black lamp from one of his many pockets. "I went back to the 1500s in Persia to get this from a bloodthirsty king. Then planted it in France on October of 1907 to birth the holiday, and I just returned from this very place in Times Square during the year 1904 for the birth of this building."

"Why this building?" the sweet woman asked, almost pleading with the ambitious young man. "You know this building is beneath the Phoenix's home in Cloud City. We shouldn't be here."

"Creating the new spirit of our holiday will be well worth it, I assure you." The young man placed the black lamp on top of a jagged piece of stone that he had pulled from his other pocket. "I needed a piece of time from history so the holiday will have a place to connect to its time of birth. Now that you're here, we can combine them and become the holiday spirit we always had the potential to be."

Considering the possibility that these were the two symbols that may have created Halloween, Jack stared on as Sonny went closer. "Where are you going?" he asked.

"To get a closer look," she replied, watching the brother and sister.

Jack tried tugging on her shirt to bring her back to no avail. "This is why people die in horror movies, you realize that?"

"Why do you need me?" asked the young woman of her brother. "You're more than capable alone, but I would urge you to go into hiding before the holiday spirits realize what you've done."

"You are my sister," said the young man as his shirt began to change magically into one similar to his sister's dress. His head and body had also changed until, soon, he resembled her exactly. "I may be a master of disguise, but without you, I am not whole or powerful enough. We were created for this purpose to be done together. This is what our master holiday has created us for, and we must follow that lead." He took her hand, morphing back into himself, and raised their hands over the lamp.

Before anything else could happen, Jack noticed Sonny's eyes dart to a wall as figures appeared one at a time entering the corridor from a blue light. At least a dozen holiday spirits, including those Jack recognized as the April Fool's spirit, Holly of Christmas, the love doctor, and a red-haired man in crimson-colored clothes, who was surely Phoenix. They surrounded the brother and sister instantly, and Holly removed her cloak and spoke boldly.

"We have spoken to Father, your inventor, and your holiday spirit and have seen how you have become uncontrollable," she called out.

"I serve my holiday spirit as he has birthed me to do so, fulfilling my purpose. And no one will stop us from doing so," replied the young man, looking at his sister for support. She tightened her grip on his hand in response.

"We will not allow you do this," said the April Fool, fumbling with something shiny in his hand. "You'll create a monster that may be impossible to stop."

"You are but a fool yourself if you think you can stop us now when we are so close." The young man's confident face was almost fully visible now. "When this is all done, they will call me the king of pranks and all mischief and have a holiday of fear. When I'm through, they will create a phobia of my holiday."

The Spirit of April Fool's Day threw a hand buzzer down at the feet of the brother and sister. It exploded, causing a shockwave in the ground that forced both siblings to laugh uncontrollably. In the commotion, the Spirit of April Fool's Day attempted to stick an expanding whoopee cushion to the brother, but he avoided it and withdrew a sword with a skull-shaped handle along with an egg from one of his pockets. The Fool instantly became invisible, dodging the thrown egg as he forced the other spirit to lose all gravity and hit the ceiling with force. A very short spirit multiplied himself, and his multiples grabbed the sister and disappeared with her before she had time to react.

"No!" yelled her brother as he fought off the April Fool's spirit. Removing a spool of toilet tissue from another pocket, he unraveled it around him and quickly vanished — but not before the April Fool's spirit collided with him and vanished as well, leaving a spiral of black smoke behind.

Almost at once, the other spirits looked at each other and vanished in a flash of blue light, leaving Jack and Sonny alone in the room.

"Where'd they go?" Jack asked Sonny.

"I believe they followed them out." Sonny froze. "Why are we still here? Is it not the end of the film?"

Searching around for the screen they had entered through, Jack tried to find an opening but couldn't. "I can't find a screen anywhere. Sam, let us out!"

After a few moments of searching in silence without a response from the usher or anyone else, Jack slumped against a wall. "We can't have more than a couple of hours left now."

"Jack, try using your flashlight," Sonny suggested. "It may be able to bend through the haze of these walls!"

Directing the light toward the inner part of the building, he began shining it over the walls. Through a small patch behind a few crates, he could see theater chairs and a projection machine — all in color. A man in the background stared through the eyepiece, smiling with a grin as wide as a jack-o'-lantern's. Calling Sonny over to him, Jack took her hand and climbed quickly through the illuminated hole in the screen. They landed with a loud thud on the floor of the theater. Their glasses had reappeared on their faces, but they were now easily removable. The usher had only now noticed that they were getting up from the floor and had left the movie when he called out.

"Hey, what are you doing? You can't leave in the middle of the movie!" the usher called out after them. They ran through the theater and into the summertime hall.

Sonny had brought out her notepad and began writing. "Do you think he'll follow us?" she asked.

They continued to the televator, where Jack pressed the key for floor forty-four. "No, I'm pretty sure he's bound to that villa."

Sonny glanced at the floor Jack had chosen. "We're going to see the Halloween spirit now, I assume?" she asked as the doors opened.

"I still think it's possible it could be Dr. de Luca, but there's not enough evidence. But Mr. Shadow fits. I can't think of any other real conclusions, except that somehow Mr. Shadow and his sister succeeded in creating the holiday that became Halloween," Jack responded. "I can't understand why they allowed him to be. Maybe once you're a holiday spirit, there's no going back, but it doesn't really matter. Mr. Shadow is either up to this or knows enough about it, and we have to find out what."

They entered a very dimly lit hall with jack-o'-lanterns smiling back at them from between each of the doors on the left side. A thin fog along with a light breeze seemed to emit from their mouths as if they were breathing. Spiderwebs dangled in corners like netting awaiting a capture, and a light moaning tingled in Sonny's and Jack's ears.

"No wonder the attendant on this floor doesn't like it here." Jack shivered.

"It's only a few spiderwebs and fog," Sonny stated, shaking her head and leading the way to the center of the right wall. She waited for Jack to join her as he turned on his flashlight. The sunspots began spinning slightly in the handle as he walked. Pointing his flashlight through the haze of the wall, they found a new stand-alone door with a full-length mirror. As their search for a handle failed, blood-red words appeared on the mirror reading "Face Your Worst Fears."

As she stared into the mirror, Sonny's face changed, as if she were looking at something truly horrifying, and she held her hands over her eyes, repeatedly saying she was in a large room.

Jack stared into the mirror as an image appeared. His father walked up from the ashes of a burning airplane that had recently crashed, asking him why he'd let him die. He told Jack that his mother would be next when he fails and that he couldn't save either of them. His father repeated this a few times before he turned into a frightening clown with sharp yellow teeth, pointed eyebrows, white skin, and red eyes, his matching his nose stabbing at the mirror.

Trying to block his face from the clown's thrashing of the mirror, Jack used the flashlight, but it didn't show anything differently. Sonny sat on the floor with her eyes closed tightly, spreading her arms out wide. The clown shook the mirror violently and began stabbing at it with a butcher knife as Jack tried using the handle of his flashlight instead. The sunspots were still spinning, but he was able to barely see a hidden handle where the clown had cracked the mirror. He placed his key card into the handle between shakes. The clown's knife disappeared, and, soon, he did as well; then the door unlocked, opening slightly.

Sonny opened her eyes and stood up shakily. "Sorry," she said, wiping a tear away. "There isn't much I'm fearful of, but a small space is one that I am. Suppose you would have to have no heart at all to be unafraid of everything."

"It's alright," Jack said as he noticed a piece of fabric on the floor. It was a red-and-brown tie like the ones the Spirit of Father's Day wore. Picking it up and placing it in his pocket, he opening the door a bit more and they entered. "We should be prepared for anything. If Mr. Shadow has Phoenix and the hourglass, we have to find a way to release him quickly."

Stepping into the Halloween spirit's villa was like stepping into a nightmare from a horror movie. The smell was repulsive, like aged meat. There was no light anywhere, but Jack could see figures moving just well enough to tell that there was someone else with them, breathing slightly as if asleep.

"Help me find a slot to turn off the security," he told Sonny.

"Why don't you turn on your flashlight?" she replied, "I believe it would be easier."

Something about the room being so dark made Jack uneasy, but, in the end, he realized she was right. It would be impossible to locate the slot without some kind of light. However, turning on the flashlight, he could clearly see a small army of skeletal creatures facing them. Their heads had all turned toward him. Hundreds of empty sockets stared dreadfully. Most had very little flesh clinging onto various parts of their bodies as they began twitching and marching their way over, calling for the holder of the light. The sound of wet, scraping bones echoed in their ears as the creatures grew closer.

"Quick! Help me find a slot!" Jack yelled out, moving as fast as possible. Yet without a flashlight of her own, as much as she tried, Sonny couldn't find much of anything in the dark. They were being quickly enclosed upon, and Sonny could feel the space closing in on her as she panicked.

"Jack, just turn it off!" She snatched his flashlight from him. Shaking it violently, she flicked the switch as the skeletons' twitching forward movement ceased and everything became dark again.

"We won't be able to find the security slot this way, and we can't move through them," Jack called out to her quietly, unable to see her in the dark. "Maybe we can split up and force them to a corner or something."

With the flashlight in her hand, Sonny made a throwing motion toward Jack. "Or maybe we can just toss it and run?" She could tell immediately that Jack didn't like that idea. However, the creatures had begun moving toward Jack again, where a small orb of very warm light had landed. Jack ran over to Sonny as the light went out completely after a few seconds, and the skeletons held their ground once more, returning to their original state.

"How did you do that?" Jack asked to Sonny's confusion. "You threw light somehow."

Sonny handed Jack's flashlight back to him. He inspected it carefully, noticing there were now only two sunspots in the handle. They were spinning faster than he had ever seen.

"It's like they're excited about dark places." He brought the flashlight as far back behind his head as he could reach. With all of his effort, he swung the flashlight as hard as he could. A ball of light flew through the air, landing many yards away on their left. The skeletons awoke and immediately gave chase, thrashing into each other and fighting to get to it. When enough of them were gone, Jack and Sonny ran to the right side, following the wall as far as they could before running into another door. This one had a no mirror. Instead, its sign read "No Tricks."

After only a glance at Sonny, Jack used his skeleton key card to open the door to a new room. Here, they witnessed the ground covered in mossy tombstones stretching as far as they could see. Large pumpkins with different faces carved into each of them followed a path leading through the field of graves. Spiders crawled in and out of giant webs in the eyes of the pumpkins, appearing to watch them as they continued. The smell of rotting flesh had left their senses and was now replaced by stale air, mold, and decaying pumpkins. Besides the moon above them, the pumpkins cast the only lights in the area with a radiant green glow from inside that was like swamp gas spewing from their grotesque, gaping grins. Following the cobblestone path, Sonny led their way through this room.

It wasn't much longer before their walk turned into a run as the pumpkins began to murmur the same chant.

"No tricks, no disguises," they repeated as the green gas began gushing from their mouths, forcing the spiders to scurry away. Soon, the path ended, but the pumpkins continued to release the green gas hastily, as if to chase Jack and Sonny through the room.

"We'll have to go onto the grass," Sonny said to Jack's dismay. Reluctantly, they jumped onto the grass, passing by tombstone after tombstone and growing closer to the end of the field, until the ground began to sink in. Before they could react, Sonny tripped over a sunken mound of dirt and landed hard. When Jack went to help her up, a corpse hand shot up from a grave like a rocket, keeping him from a reaching her even though she was only a foot or so away.

They were held in one spot long enough for the green gas to catch up to them and begin melting their attendant uniforms away from them both. Their coats, shoes, hats, and pants all dissolved, but their regular clothes beneath were untouched. Everything they carried with them, including Sonny's notepad, pen, the Blueberry Fiz, her gift from Holly, and Jack's flashlight had gone unharmed. The ground became solid again, releasing Sonny from its surface as the hand retreated to its grave and freed Jack from its clutch, when Sonny began coughing frantically.

"Sonny, what's . . . what's?" Jack fell to the ground, holding his throat and gasping for air. Every breath he attempted pulled in nothing, as if he were drowning without water. He could feel his heart thump harder in his chest, aching for oxygen. His lungs were squeezed like an accordion, forcing out his remaining air. He reached for something, anything to help him breathe. Sonny had fallen, too, and her eyes began to roll back. They were only inches away from each other, now, as Jack crawled over to her, realizing the gas had gotten into their lungs. Trying his hardest to fight the urge to give up, he stopped crawling and grabbed at anything he could until he could go no farther. He was clutching in his hand two small objects he assumed were rocks.

Taking a last look up at the moon, he reached up, his skin turning a pale-green hue, hoping someone would save them like in his dream. As he opened his hand, reaching toward the sky, two small wrapped items he had forgotten

Sonny was given fell onto his chest. He realized what he had grabbed from the ground had fallen from her pocket, and his hopes rose slightly. He unwrapped red plastic from the heart-shaped chocolate, and he placed it into his mouth, feeling its sweet, delectable cocoa create a small opening for him to breathe through. As he gasped for air, he crawled over to Sonny's unmoving body and unwrapped the other chocolate. He scrambled to place it into her mouth, but she still hadn't moved.

"Come on, Sonny, wake up. You gotta stop leaving me like this all the time. I can't do this alone, and I can't lose anyone else," Jack said, waiting patiently with his head in his hands. Her face had turned a pale green, and Jack lost hope, believing he had been too late. Her notepad, pen, and Fiz drink were lying next to her, just as still as she.

A strong gasp for air forced Jack to raise his head up as Sonny began to regain her natural skin tone. She began to move her mouth around, tasting what was left of the candy. "Eww, I'm not fond of chocolate," she said with a sour face.

Jack couldn't help but smile. "Well, you should stop lying down on the job all the time, then. Or we'll never get anything done."

The green gas from the pumpkins' eerie smiles lingered in the air as Jack helped Sonny up, yet they seemed immune to the effects after eating the doctor's chocolate. After gathering up their items and climbing up a hill through the field of tombstones, they approached another stone path leading to a third door. It was black with candy apples framing the outside, sugar sprinkled on the front, and a vampire cookie on the key slot. A sign written in red above this stated "No Treats."

Taking a deep breath, Jack placed his key card into the door slot, where the vampire cookie bit down onto it. Once it was accepted, the door opened and released the card, allowing them inside. Upon entering this room, the door closed behind them and locked instantly. This room was much smaller than the others had been. Only a single podium and a small, basketball-sized black cauldron that sat atop it were clearly visible sitting in front of two tall covered cages. Strangely, it reminded Jack of his dream about the creepy game show host as they grew closer to it. There was nothing inside it. Jack read a small white card in front of the cauldron. "A werewolf shakes cages, waiting for you. A vengeful spirit will haunt your mind. A single candy will appear for you two. If correct, will rescue in time."

Once they had finished reading, a green countdown from fifteen developed above the cauldron as the cages were exposed. The cage to their left shook violently as a creature twice their size stared at them with yellow eyes as if they were rare treat. His fangs drooled menacingly as he clawed at Sonny and Jack, reaching within inches of their faces. As they smelled the fresh blood on his breath and fur, they knew the werewolf was not far from breaking free.

The spirit in the right cage was just as terrifying; it was unlike any of the spirits staying in the hotel. A translucent figure with a slight green glow from the clock wore a straitjacket and had long, shaggy hair. The chains binding him rattled and dragged on the ground as if ready to break as well, but it was easy to tell they wouldn't need to. Even still locked away, he began placing their worst fears and nightmares into their minds, making it impossible for them to concentrate.

"You're a bright one," Sonny said, turning to Jack as the clock reached twelve seconds. "What's the answer?"

Jack couldn't think clearly, feeling the air wave past him as the beast clawed. He was seeing fragments of his father as a clown then as himself flying in an airplane. "I don't know. . . . I need more time." He began to back away, attempting to bring Sonny with him.

Only eight seconds remained as he watched her put a hand to her temple, thinking hard. Almost at once, she removed the Blueberry Fiz from her pocket and drank about half the bottle. With two seconds left, the cages began to bend and twist and the spirit's chains were loosening.

"A Life Saver!" Sonny shouted out. The cages burst open as the candy filled the cauldron; she grabbed one for each of them before the werewolf ran through, clawing harshly and destroying the podium. The cauldron spilled and candy spread everywhere. She tossed a piece of candy to Jack and ate one herself as Jack hoped she was correct. Once they placed the candy into their mouths, both the spirit and the werewolf ceased to move. The spirit, ready to fly at them, let out a ghastly moan that was followed by a final howl from the werewolf before they both faded away.

A final door appeared behind the podium, this time with no sign—just a crystal door knocker in the shape of a gargoyle. And the door was already unlocked and ajar. The door led to the steep staircase of a castle's archway. Lightning struck across the sky, creating shadows of the bare trees. The villa wasn't as haunting as Jack had thought it'd be. The walls were made of dark gray bricks. It had a violet roof and large bay windows. It was elegant but still uninviting. From the stone towers to the castle itself, only one window remained lit. Neither of them said a word as they climbed each step and grew closer to finding Mr. Shadow. After fighting through all the security and almost dying, they had made it to the archway of the castle. A long hallway with a lengthy black rug on the floor lay in front of them, leading to a single throne. A man stared from the throne as they entered, his hands laying on the armrests as if he had been waiting for them for some time now. A fire danced behind, him making most of his body appear shaded. His shadow seemed to move on its own. It stood to the man's side with its arms folded, tapping its foot.

Jack and Sonny stepped inside carefully, unsure of what surprises may be left. The closer they drew to the man, noticing his perfectly pressed black suit with a black silk shirt and crimson-red tie, the more they realized he didn't look like anyone they had seen previously. He seemed slender and muscular, much like an older version of the young man they'd seen in the movie but with more dignity. Jack wasn't sure if other holiday spirits besides Phoenix aged, but this spirit appeared much older than the young man they'd seen in the film. A black, hooded cloak lay at his feet as he motioned them forward with a pale finger.

"We know you're the one behind the missing holidays, Shadow," Jack stated boldly. "We've seen the moments leading up to the dark holiday and you with your sister. Where are they, and what have you done with the owner?!"

The spirit hadn't moved much at all, but they could sense the room growing colder without warning. The same strong sense of fear tingled their senses. It was difficult, but Sonny tried to shake it off as best she could.

"We watched you and your sister create Halloween and try to become a holiday spirit," Sonny stated bravely. "We have enough to prove to the manager it was you this time. You were sneaking up to the first floor, we found Father's tie outside your villa, and you're the only holiday spirit removed from the books as if you are not a holiday spirit at all. Like you and your sister were only a holiday spirit's symbols."

"Quite alarming, kid," said the spirit in a cold, cruel yet smooth voice. Each word sent chills as he spoke, as if he could pierce the worst thoughts into their minds. His shadow walked the edges of the room as the spirit spoke. "Through all of your research, you came to a conclusion that the obvious dark holiday would be Halloween and the spirit would, of course, be me? I did hope you would be brighter than the others, but you are just as closed-minded as everyone else. Your obviously insulting demeanor and intrusion into my villa has proven that you are nothing but children in a mess too large for your feeble and inferior minds to comprehend. The dark holiday was never Halloween. I am the holiday spirit the two symbols reported to. The twin symbols were creating a day of bad luck and misfortune through drastically dark and dreadful events bestowed upon everyone who would come to witness it . . . Friday the Thirteenth."

# Chapter 10
## *The Joker*

$\mathcal{M}$r. Shadow's castle seemed to represent him very well as he continued to be as condescending as possible. Although it was very clean, it appeared to be cold and uninviting, as if no one had cared for it in many years and outsiders were not welcome. The mantel above the fireplace held picture frames with no photos. Silence seemed to echo from the numerous rooms throughout the castle, and Mr. Shadow seemed to prefer his solitude as he brought them into the study. A seemingly infinite number of books lined the walls from the floor to the ceiling on oak shelves. Mr. Shadow sat carefully into an armchair, as if there were never a reason to rush for anything. Sitting across from him, Sonny took notes as Jack questioned the Halloween spirit as thoroughly as he could.

"What do you mean Friday the Thirteenth?" Jack was unsure if he believed anything the spirit said. "Two symbols were involved with the dark holiday and Father already went missing, leaving you as the likely spirit."

Mr. Shadow's eyes appeared to narrow in the darkness over his face. "I'm beginning to wonder if you are much brighter than the ones who condemned me in the first place. So many like you only hear or see half-truths, believing it all without truly investigating."

"So what is the truth?" Sonny asked. "What is the real history? Who really created the dark holiday?"

The spirit released a large sigh in Sonny's direction. "Decades ago, the Spirit of Father's Day created the first few holiday symbols. They served many purposes but, overall, to protect and enhance a holiday, which in turn heightened its popularity. The more a holiday spirit is celebrated, the more powerful they become. For some time, many referred to my holiday as dark and a worship of the dead, instead of a celebration of those who had passed. I knew All Hollow's Eve could be so much more, so he created two symbols from my personality."

No one said a word as the spirit spoke. Jack could tell Sonny was attempting, just as he was, to remember what symbols Halloween had. The room grew darker as a cloud hid the moon outside, and Mr. Shadow continued. "They were brother and sister born from my personality at the same moment. One from my generosity to celebrate and be giving, the other from my cunning and adventuring."

"I don't think I've ever heard of any symbols for this holiday," Jack stated.

"Do thoughts ever appear in your mind fully before you speak. . . . No?" asked Mr. Shadow coldly. "On All

Hollow's Eve, after your ridiculous costumes and childish horror stories, when you knock on a door expecting your teeth-rotting delights, you call their names. . . . Treat was a very sweet girl, providing candy and treats for many. Her brother, Trick, however, turned out to be more trouble than we'd ever imagined."

"Trick and Treat were your symbols?" Jack asked as Sonny stopped writing momentarily.

"Is your hearing an issue as well?" The spirit raised his voice slightly. "Or is time no longer an issue for you? Because I would very much like to continue *uninterrupted* so I may finish my last moments in this world alone, as I find myself with the only intelligent thoughts in the room."

Although it was difficult, Jack fought the urge to respond and remained quiet. Mr. Shadow proceeded. "Trick was very determined and ambitious. He had a talent for manipulating the shadows in different ways. It wasn't long before he could use it to travel short distances, always looking for something challenging to do. I believe it was the fearless adventure he was created with that enthralled him. Decades passed with no issues. Without my knowledge, he created an adapted holiday in my honor. It was Mischief Night. No symbol has ever been able to do so. I was very proud. However, there are rules, and without the blessing of the seasons, it is forbidden to spawn new holidays. The holiday became a conflict with April Fool's Day being too similar. Trick became outraged."

Sonny scribbled so fast that Jack thought she would burn holes into the walls when the writing appeared in the hotel room. They continued listening intently, not daring to speak as Mr. Shadow carried on with his story.

"Trick attempted to out-prank the April Fool's spirit with his millennium prank. Although we were able to stop the occurrence, it took months to prove it was him when the evidence pointed to me. After it was all finished, many of the others believed I had put him up to it, and some even think Father assisted me in that aspect by creating them. That is why I no longer leave my villa, even to go home, unless it's for my holiday. On Friday, October thirteenth, 2000, we were able to stop him from being developed into a full holiday spirit, although it was too late to stop the holiday. To this day, its effects still haunt us. Ironically, we were lucky this holiday of misfortune hadn't reached its full power by gaining a spirit."

Mr. Shadow waved his hand in a circle as black smoke formed into a goblet. He took a sip from the goblet and placed it onto a stand next to him. Jack noticed how elderly his hands appeared beneath the darkness. He was surprised when Sonny spoke up.

"Excuse me, sir," she said with her pen in the air like a reporter working for a news team at a press conference. "How exactly did you stop Trick? During the history film, everyone disappeared and that was the end."

The spirit waved the goblet away and sat in silence for a moment. "The game of the year," he said to Jack and Sonny as they became truly confused, "A device based on the calendar year, created by the April Fool's spirit to trap the symbol. The four seasons leading to the weeks of the year are all included. It was the only way we could contain him until he was sent to trial, judged, and sentenced." Sonny swallowed, but the spirit waved it off. "He wasn't destroyed, although maybe he should have been. He and his sister were sent to two separate inescapable containment centers deep beneath two small islands separated by a larger island. Trick was escorted there by the April Fool's Day spirit himself to ensure his containment. On this island, the captives are watched by some very unique people with unbelievable abilities, able to see all they are doing at this very moment and what they will do in the future."

Mr. Shadow looked through one of his windows and stared into the sky at the moon. "Now, your time is up. There's less than an hour left before midnight, and whatever hope I had for you to succeed has clearly been misrepresented. I disabled the security, so you may see yourselves out."

Standing up to excuse herself, Sonny closed her notepad and placed it and her pen into her back pocket. Though he was sure it would lead to yet another insult from the spirit, there was a question that had plagued Jack and that he had to ask.

"I have one last question I must ask you," he said as respectfully as possible, though with restraint. "Treat provided sweets as the symbol of Halloween, and you already had a celebration for death, so horror was taken care of. What exactly was Trick's purpose for Halloween?"

The chills began to seep into his skin and down his spine as Mr. Shadow stood up. Sonny glanced around the room as it grew steadily darker before Mr. Shadow spoke once more. "He was a master of disguise and could change forms at any time to look like anyone he wanted for as long as he wanted. One of the ways he chose to use the gift of shadow was to create masks. I, however, prefer more delicate measures, like this." With a snap of the spirit's fingers, Jack felt weightless as a dark substance appeared around his ankles. Immediately, he and Sonny were transported back outside of the castle hall to the top of the stairs. The clouds separated from the moon, casting a glow on Sonny's gift sitting next to her. The tree branches were no longer waving in the wind and were now very still, as if they knew the end was near. A door appeared from the shadows at the top of the staircase, blocking entry into the castle.

Bringing out his flashlight, Jack turned it on and focused it on the door to the next room as he continued down the stairs. After picking up her gift from Holly, Sonny followed him down as well, not speaking until they reached the bottom.

"Are we heading back to our floor?" she asked as they opened the door leading to the trick-or-treat-riddle room.

The motionless cages no longer rattled as Jack went by with determination. "You're good with plans, and I have an idea, but it doesn't make much sense yet." Jack crossed into the next room. "If you're with me on this, it all fits together, though. . . . Does that make sense?"

"Nonsense or not, I'm sure we both know I'm staying around," Sonny responded casually. "Sometimes a ridiculous idea can lead to a brilliant one."

"Well, Trick can disguise himself like he did turning into his sister in the film, then maybe that's what he's been doing all along," Jack said as they reached the exit into the graveyard. "But how could he escape an inescapable island being watched by those who can see the future of their captives, unless . . ."

"Unless he was never really captured," Sonny concluded, stepping over the now-silent pumpkins in the graveyard. "That would explain how the April Fool's spirit changed his head into a false Mr. Shadow. When the April Fool's spirit escorted him to the island, Trick must've switched with him and has been posing for the last twelve years."

"In less than an hour it'll be thirteen years since the new millennium," stated Jack as they trudged through the graveyard. "Perfect timing for Friday the Thirteenth. Faking his own disappearance was the perfect way to keep guests in their rooms while he searched for the hourglass."

"And what about Father?" Sonny asked as they entered the first room. The skeletal figures were huddled in a corner, standing very still.

They had reached the door with the fear mirror as Jack turned to Sonny. "That's why we need to reach the April Fool's Day villa. It's possible Trick grew a hatred for the Father's Day spirit for creating the year-based game trap. Only downfall to all of this is, the hourglass may not be there, and if he's hiding, he could very well be any of the fifty-two attendants."

After reaching the televator and taking it to the fourteenth floor, Jack used the handle of his flashlight to examine the floor. Sonny kept a lookout for anyone who may come by now that they had no attendant uniforms for disguises. The hallway with its spring colors had gone unchanged, but the floor itself held a tan, glistening path leading to Jack's room, Sonny's room, and the wall across from them. Bending down to touch a small amount of it and placing it under his nose, he inhaled slightly and began yawning. "It's the same sand," he said, handing the flashlight to Sonny.

After inspecting the path through the lens, Sonny handed the flashlight back. "How do you know it's not different sand?" she asked. "They all appeared the same before."

Jack stood up and began walking toward the center of the blank wall. "It's the dream sand from the Phoenix's villa on the roof. That's why it makes me yawn. It's the same sand that caused you to fall asleep. I figured there would be trails leading to our rooms because we were in the villa, but it also leads to this wall." He examined the wall carefully. Grabbing Sonny's hand in his left and his flashlight in his right, he stepped through the wall. "When Mr. Shadow mentioned Trick was a master of disguise, I remembered the April Fool's spirit morphing his head into Mr. Shadow's, just like he did his sister's in the film."

"So, how do you know Trick hasn't posed as another spirit?" Sonny removed her notepad and flipped through pages, clicking her pen.

A mirror similar to the one for the Halloween villa's door guarded the April Fool's Day spirit's villa. "Because posing as attendants is exactly what we did, making it easy to move about without being noticed."

The mirror curved like a fun house's, displaying strange reflections of them both. Sonny snickered at her elongated face, and a slot appeared near the edge of the door, but it was difficult to see. Jack tilted his head, and, using the flashlight's light, inserted his skeleton key card into it. As the door opened, Jack shuddered. It was eerily similar to a funhouse, strongly reminding Jack of his father turning into a clown in the fear mirror. They could hear the soft sound of carnival music skipping and repeating as if it were on a broken record player. Mirrors lined the walls encircling them. There was no exit except the way they had come in.

"Looks to be a dead end, and I don't see a slot for the alarm," Sonny stated, searching the mirrors closely. Jack tried using his flashlight handle and the light to find anything helpful, but it seemed to have no effect. As Sonny went from one mirror to the next, her reflection appeared determined to linger in a mirror, giggling and then jumping to the next shortly after. Sonny followed it around the room with her eyes until it stood behind Jack. Jack's reflection in front of him stayed still, as if studying him. From across the room, Sonny's reflection reached into her back pocket and threw something at Jack's head. When he turned around, the reflection vanished. A notepad like Sonny's flopped on the ground and then, shortly after, vanished as well. Jack stood rubbing his head until Sonny went over to the mirror on the far left.

"Hmm. . . . That's interesting." She drew a picture into her notepad and held it up to the mirror. After pressing it against the mirror, she removed it as a knob appeared. "Not sure how long it will last, so we should probably go now." She tried reaching for it, but she couldn't touch anything except the mirror itself.

Jack started walking toward it, and his reflection followed. After watching Jack grow closer as his reflection drew farther away and almost walked away from view, Sonny stopped him. "Wait, you're going too far away. You should go around the room and bring your reflection with you to open the door, or I think he'll go away for good."

Jack turned to his reflection, who seemed to smirk at him as if agreeing with her. So he did as instructed and followed the mirrors in a circle until reaching the doorknob, which had already begun to fade. Jack made a twisting motion with his hand, and his reflection followed and turned the doorknob, opening the mirror to a new room.

"This is why you make the plans," Jack said, entering the new room. Sonny followed until they were in a narrow, dark area. Although it was difficult to see, they could hear the sound of air inflating something in the distance. It was followed by something sparking like wires shorting out and burning smells. Jack tried to turn on his flashlight, but before he could, he slipped and fell down a long, broad slide. Flashes of light struck behind and in front of him on either side as he plummeted down the steep slope and realized there were hand buzzers on the sides. They began charging and then lit up with electricity just as he passed by, singeing his fingers slightly. He tried spreading his hands and fingers apart as much as possible to slow himself down, but the incline was too great.

Finally, passing by the last smoking buzzer, he barely made it to the bottom before the blue light started again and singed his hair. Planting his feet on the ground, he heard another sound that startled him. Sonny was coming down fast, but she wasn't fast enough as a side sparked up. The blue light of the hand buzzer illuminated and charged up until a line of electricity had been drawn.

"Sonny, jump when you hit the lip!" he called out to her. The line of electricity danced in front of Jack as if already claiming victory. Not a full second had passed when Sonny planted her feet down and leaped over the electricity. Jack caught her as she landed, unharmed, atop him.

"Nice caaatch!" Sonny yelled as they were both dropped deep into what seemed to be a pink ball pit, though it was difficult to tell in the dark. They had been separated by a few feet but were otherwise unharmed. The soft rubber cushioned their landings with little effort.

"Can something *not* happen to us for a little while?" Jack said, searching for an exit as a hissing sound echoed in the area. The sound of something inflating had returned, but

Jack was focused on other situations. On a ledge above him, a corridor led to another door that Jack could barely see. "Up there, I see a door. We just have to figure out how to get to it." He pointed.

"Uh, Jack," Sonny said, sounding worried. "That may no longer be the only problem we have."

As Jack looked back at her, he realized the ball pit they had landed in was actually not a ball pit at all, but a pit filled with inflating whoopee cushions. They were growing to gargantuan size, decreasing the space greatly. Before long, the cushions had squeezed them to the sides, sticking to them so that they were unable to move and were pinned against the walls.

"Jack, use your flashlight for the last smmmm," she mumbled as the pink rubber covered her face.

"What?!" Jack asked, shouting over the noise. Reaching for his flashlight, he tried to figure out what Sonny was trying to say as whoopee cushions pinned his right arm down. Using his left arm, he raised his flashlight in the air and noticed the last sun spot inside spinning around as it craved the dark. He remembered how warm it was when he had used it in the Halloween villa. Reaching as high as he could, he flicked the flashlight, and a ball of light shot into the air and landed on a whoopee cushion that was pinning his head down. A sound like a popping car tire could be heard all around as the light burned holes into the rubber. Soon, Jack's arm was free, and he could see Sonny climbing up the pink rubber. She leaped from it toward him.

"Hurry!" he yelled, using an inflated cushion to climb onto a ledge.

After pulling himself up, he reached out a hand for Sonny, who was rising quickly to the top as the ball of light went out. Jack managed to pull her onto the ledge before the whoopee cushions filled the space to the ceiling. Jack used his skeleton key card to unlock the door in front of them. Once safely inside, he closed the door and leaned against it as a loud explosion of air caused by the whoopee cushions filling to maximum size shook the room.

They couldn't help but smile at the sound it made after their narrow escape. Looking about their new surroundings, Jack wasn't sure if he was delighted or disturbed. The walls were pure white but splattered with red writing, similar to Sonny's room. Two phrases repeated several times: "The Dark Holiday is coming" and "I am the prank KING!" A few others cursed the Father's Day spirit and the April Fool's Day spirit. A single photo of Treat with Trick smiling mischievously sat on a high shelf. Besides the large amount of dream sand and pieces of yellow caution tape laying everywhere, Jack found only a few crimson strands through his flashlight's handle but no hourglass.

"Where is he?" Sonny asked, searching every space she could. She found a staircase in a corner, but even it was bare.

"He must still be searching for the hourglass too, or he's with the attendants." Jack was looking for other clues when he paused. "How much time do we have?" he asked Sonny.

Pulling out her notepad and pen, she asked the question and received an immediate response. "We have twelve minutes until midnight," she said with wide eyes.

Hoping they would be in time, Jack looked back at her, debating whether he should go to the top floor or to the bottom floor. After looking at the floor, he decided. "We've gotta get down to the fifty-second floor, now." They used the staircase in the corner of the room that led them back to the fourteenth floor, and they took the televator down to the ground floor. He was somewhat worried the attendants would stop them the moment they stepped out. However, with so little time, he knew they had to take the risk.

As he exited the televator, Jack noticed that the water from the fountain had turned completely black. It flowed slowly like tar, as if every last remaining second of time flowed with it. A few tourists and the attendants were huddled in a small circle when Emanuel emerged from the center, pointing in their direction. Four attendants rushed over to them and restrained Jack and Sonny. Jack noticed the yellow tape on Number Forty-Three's shoe as she held Sonny's arm and Number Fifty-Two stood by the door.

"Wait! We know who has the hourglass!" Jack said over the commotion. The attendants froze, staring at Number One, looking for guidance.

"That's not possible," Emanuel said with dignity, dividing the attendants as he walked toward Jack and Sonny. "Where is it?"

The attendants loosened their grip on Jack. He fumbled for his flashlight and then looked through the handle. "We found out who had the hourglass by following the right clues." Jack was thinking hard, scanning the room. "After we spoke to the Spirit of Father's Day, we heard a loud thump and two people laughing—a man and a woman. It wasn't much longer before we found out Father had gone missing, but now we know someone had the ability to pose as Mother, allowing entrance into Father's villa."

The crowd of attendants followed him as he moved about, speaking. "After meeting Usher Sam and seeing the imposter Mr. Shadow, it was easy to tie them all to the

~ 191 ~

symbol Trick with a single common trait. They each smiled like a jack-o'-lantern . . . which I also noticed on one other person in this room—someone who had an issue with yellow tape," he said, glaring at Number Forty-Three. Number Fifty-Two stood by the door, looking between them intently. When Jack eyed his direction, his mouth opened wide.

The manager stopped Jack. "I've had enough of this nonsense. With only a few minutes left before midnight, you waste the time we could be using to search for the hourglass, and you clearly have no idea of its whereabouts. I will not stand by as you accuse one of my employees."

"But I do know," Jack said as the attendants grabbed him again, pulling him away. "The hourglass was hidden by the very first person who spoke to me when I entered the hotel." Many attendants and Sonny looked at Number Fifty-Two, and some looked at the manager, unsure whom he had spoken to first. However, Jack pointed to someone else entirely. "The elderly man in the crimson-red pajamas is Phoenix." A few people stared at the white-haired man as if not believing it was possible he'd been there the whole time.

"I overheard a few attendants discussing how strong the New Year's spirit was and that it'd be impossible to overpower him. After I found out no other holidays aged except Phoenix and with the end of the year so near, I knew he would be in his old age. He's the only one here who looks elderly. He went easily unnoticed since no one ever sees him grow up, only seeing his appearance the first and last day of his new form. No one would know what he looks like. I assume he simply wandered out of his room and didn't know how to get back. That's why his door was open and there was no damage on it. Probably led out by someone posing as a friend in search of the hourglass who hadn't realized Phoenix hid it elsewhere," Jack stated, looking at Number Forty-Three. "Someone who has made a few too many mistakes," he continued, walking over to the manager's podium.

"Someone stop him!" yelled Number One as Jack opened the door behind the desk. It revealed a few black bags like the one Emanuel had carried on Jack's first full day of the hotel, but they had become smaller, fitting well behind the wall.

Jack turned to the attentive listeners. "There's only one floor where an attendant hasn't been stationed lately. After Sonny overheard a phone hang up on our floor from the Spirit in the April Fool's villa, I remembered Emanuel answering a call from the owner, who hasn't been heard from in days. When he returned, smiling in that familiar way, Sonny called him 'Manny.' And he didn't correct her as he normally would. He looked as if he had been in a bad fight and was carrying a black bag like these. He stated he had cleaned up the yellow tape from the first floor. Seemed odd there was so much left there when we investigated it, and now I know why." He shined the flashlight's light on the bag, bending the haze and displaying smaller versions of the people in each of the bags, one of whom was Emanuel. "Many of the spirits here were involved and would seem guilty because they've all been used as disguises."

A few attendants rushed to the bags and removed the ties, causing the bags to enlarge. A fully grown manager crawled out. As the others were untied, the manager was followed out by an unfamiliar attendant, the Spirit of Father's Day, and Usher Sam.

"He is an imposter." The manager, who was now being encircled by the attendants, pointed at the man who had just emerged from the bag. "The dreamer is trying to

~ 193 ~

frame me. He's probably Trick, trying to confuse us."
Watching Father climb out of the bag, he seemed to realize no
one believed him. He smiled broadly, and then sprinted
toward the entrance. Shadows tangled around his ankles and
then his body with each stride until it had engulfed him
completely. Trick exited the shadows just as he had in the
film. He was now fully back to his natural form. The cunning
smirk on his face increased as he strolled over to the elderly
man. Trick's pumpkin sword hung in its scabbard at his side
as he approached. The attendants gathered around Phoenix
to protect him from the Halloween symbol as Jack ran over to
Sonny.

    "Why did you tell him who Phoenix was?" she asked,
writing a question in her notepad. She held it up for Jack to
see. "We only have four minutes left until midnight."

    "I had to stall until I could scan the attendants with the
flashlight to be sure which one was Trick," Jack explained,
checking behind him. Trick was attacking the attendants with
his egg bombs and threatening them with his pumpkin
sword. He was incredibly agile as he vanished into the
shadows and leaped out of the black smoke that had
appeared behind an attendant. The gift from Holly fell from
Sonny's hand as she tried to write. Jack witnessed more
attendants rush in from the west hall to aid in defending
Phoenix. "I need you to ask your pad what the game trap is.
If we're lucky, it may be in there."

    Sonny wrote quickly on her pad but also stared at the
gift as if she'd forgotten she were holding it. Trick took out
several attendants at once. The Spirit of Father's Day had
joined in, using a few of his gadgets to hold Trick back. A tie
flew from his neck, grappling Trick's leg. Then another seized
his arm, until the ties were swarming like snakes. When

Sonny finished writing, they waited for the answer to appear, but they were interrupted when Trick vanished in a spiraling array of toilet tissue and reappeared across the room between Jack and Sonny, blasting them away from each other.

"I hope you didn't think I'd forgotten about you two investigators," Trick said snidely, walking toward Jack.

Sonny's pad had landed next to Jack. He scooted back from Trick as he read the pad's answer as quickly as he could.

"A trap made to look like a game representing the year. The four seasons in suit will bind him. The three hundred-sixty-five spots of the year will fill gaps. Twelve faces for every month will guard. Thirteen tricks for every quarterly year to stop the dark holiday. The blank ones will split him in two, symbolizing the division of power from the twins. These fifty-two contain the power over the week to be the weapon of choice."

After reading the notepad, one line in particular stuck out. *These fifty-two contain the power over the week to be the weapon of choice,* Jack thought to himself. "Power over the week" didn't make much sense. The word meaning the opposite of powerful is spelled weak, unlike the other word referring to a calendar week. The number fifty-two only made him think more about the amount of attendants left swarming toward Trick. That's when Jack stood up and backed as far away from Trick as he could. He was confident what the weapon was. Sonny sat up in a corner, reading a card she had pulled out of her gift box. With her eyes closed, she seemed to be praying.

"Sonny, it's a deck of cards!" Jack yelled out to her. "We have to find a card deck!"

Opening her eyes, she smacked her palm against her head as Trick reached into one of his pockets, pulled out a can of spray paint, and held it up to Jack. He squeezed the nozzle, and green, blue, and orange flames spewed out as Jack ducked under the manager's podium. The flames scorched the walls and podium, leaving a few decorative plants ablaze. When the fire had stopped, Jack leaped over it, running toward Sonny as she pulled a deck of cards from the gift box and tossed it to Jack. He was confused about how she had produced the deck so quickly, but he had no time to question it. The remaining attendants, including Number Fifty-Two, tried their best to hold Trick back, but he fought them off with ease.

Jack quickly unraveled the packaging, scanning the deck of cards that appeared to be average. "I don't know what to do with them," he said, searching through the deck. "Is there a command or what?"

Time seemed to slow down immensely and tick away speedily at the same moment as an explosion went off behind Jack. A deafening shot that caused him to freeze in place flung debris in every direction. Trick appeared to be closing the gap between them, vanishing and reappearing closer to Phoenix, then closer to Jack as he laughed cruelly, bragging about the lack of time. He occasionally morphed into an attendant while tackling one, confusing them all as to who was who.

It wasn't until he heard Sonny's voice over it all that he came back from being dazed. "Find a way to get *lid o la poker!*" Sonny seemed to yell over the noise. Only three attendants were left along with Father as the real manager was hit in the head with the handle of Trick's sword and was knocked out. Jack strained to hear Sonny. As his focus narrowed, he could hear her clearly yell, "Get rid of this Joker!" She pointed to Trick.

Trick appeared over him, pulling his sword high in the air with a malicious smirk and narrow eyes, as Jack searched through the deck as quickly as he could. As Trick swung the sword down firmly, Sonny plunged her pen into his leg, causing him to jump back in pain. Thanks to her distraction, Jack found the two blank cards and dropped the rest of the deck.

Sonny backed away as Trick rounded on her. "You know, my dear, I have the ability to see fears that you may not even be aware you have," stated Trick as his he limped toward her. His sword scraped the ground as he dragged it in her direction and then raised the blade to within inches of her throat. "I've seen your mother, and she has never been happier since the day she left." Sonny's mouth fell open as she continued to glare at Trick. "Between you and your pathetic friend crying over his poor father, I'm not sure who I'm more disgusted with." Trick drew his sword back behind him like a batter ready to swing. "Suppose it is your misfortune I've grown tired of these ridiculous games!"

"How about a card trick?" Jack thought back to the first night in the hotel with his mother. He flicked his wrist and let the pair of cards fly through the air as Trick prepared to swing his sword.

White light began funneling around Trick, pulling him down and away from Sonny. Through the light, Jack could almost see his Trick's agonized face as he clawed at the ground and was sucked down into the blank cards. Once young and charming, he now appeared twisted by his insanity. His head and face began to split apart, throwing two voices as he screamed, "You'll never return the hourglass in time! The world will end, and you will see me as the prank king!" With his last words, the bright light flickered, splitting him completely in half, leaving a few wafts of smoke and two joker cards lying on the ground.

Sonny pulled the elderly man over to Jack, showing him the time left on her pad. "Jack, we have to go, there's only forty-four seconds left." Sonny urged Jack, "Where do you think he has the hourglass?"

People were beginning to stand up, staggering through the rubble all around, to focus on the cards on the ground. "It's around his neck. We have to get him to his throne," Jack said, rushing to the televator. "How did you get a deck of cards so fast?"

Sonny brought the confused Phoenix into the televator as the Father's Day spirit guarded the cards, glaring intently at them. "Holly's gift was a wish for any physical gift. So when you said a deck of cards, I wished for it." She pressed the button for the first floor.

The televator opened, revealing the now-pitch-black floor. The clocks couldn't be seen until Jack, walking hastily, shined his flashlight on them.

"Twenty-seven seconds!" he said, locating the door in the wall. The wind blew down on them harshly in the narrow staircase. He could almost hear the echoes of the past counting down from ten as the new year approached. Half carrying, half dragging the elderly spirit through the trap door of the roof, Sonny climbed through the last door and raced to the crimson-cushioned chair.

That's when Jack heard it, only a few feet away from the throne, the sound of every clock stopping all at once, attempting to continue but unable to move forward. The final tick echoed, causing him to tremble. His body felt like it had in Maurice's garden, paralyzing him again. Sonny had frozen, as well, in the act of pushing the spirit over to his throne; she was unable to move any farther. Finally, the New Year's spirit took a last breath, and as he closed his eyes, he collapsed over the armrest. His thin gold necklace with a small hourglass filled with white sand dangled from his neck as he died on the spot.

# Chapter 11
## A Secret Door

$\mathcal{B}$irds no longer flapped their wings, but instead were unmoving in the air, hovering by a cloud as if they were in a portrait of the sky. Far below the rooftop, no cars moved; people no longer rushed from store to store buying gifts or even blinked. Their faces were frozen in permanent grins, questioning glares, and disappointed frowns, and some were completely blank. However, up on the roof, a small amount of movement came from the dangling necklace of the Spirit of New Year's. It hovered over the throne, circling like a vulture ready to strike. And the last grain of sand fell into the bottom of the hourglass.

Like a compass, the hourglass began pointing directly to the center of the throne. The crimson cushion pulled it away from the neck of the spirit as if the throne were calling for the necklace. A gold glow encased the chair and then the necklace. Soon, the New Year's spirit himself was engulfed in a golden glow as Sonny's outstretched, paper-cut fingertips began to waver. Before long, her hand regained motion, stretching out for the spirit. Jack's hands followed. As they stretched their arms out, still trying to get Phoenix to his throne, a sound sparked through the sky as if all sound had started again at once.

The glow around the spirit encased him in fire as Jack and Sonny, now able to finally move again, witnessed in horror. A scream of agony and pain erupted from the spirit. Sonny covered her mouth as they both watched the Phoenix, in flames, rise into the air, forming a small ball that hovered over the throne's seat as if taking its place on the cushion. The screaming stopped as the fire died down; Jack could clearly hear the scream being replaced by giggling from what remained. As the embers died out, a baby in a diaper sat up in the throne, smiling a toothless grin.

"I believe we actually made it." Sonny smiled in astonishment at an adorable baby boy sitting in front of her.

"I can't believe he has to go through this every year," Jack said, staring at the necklace around the baby's neck. It had been refilled to the top and sand was now trickling down with the passage of time. The gold chain twinkled in the baby's eyes as he blinked twice. Suddenly, the overturned tables and chairs began moving on their own, straightening themselves up in equal distances apart. The dance floor became stunning again as the yellow tape peeled itself from the floor. Glass chandeliers repositioned themselves to hover high above the floor, and music coursed through the air from nowhere. Food and filled glasses appeared onto the tables.

Decorations hung above, bringing in the New Year's with poppers going off randomly.

"It is quite beautiful here in the moonlight," Sonny said, looking up at the sky.

Staring at the baby, Jack wondered when he would be able to see his father now that everything seemed in order. "The only thing it's missing is people," Jack stated as baby Phoenix blinked twice again, and the room filled with the guests from the hotel. The Spirit of Mother's Day appeared to be bragging to Dr. de Luca, the Valentine's Day spirit, about her gifts. A group from the Shamrock Lounge surrounded another spirit complaining about his lucky streak being over. Holly, the Spirit of Christmas, appeared to be having a conversation with baby Phoenix. Although he wasn't speaking, he seemed to understand every word she said.

There were many spirits whom Jack didn't recognize being served by the attendants. He did notice that Mr. Shadow was nowhere to be found. Although Jack wasn't surprised by this, a small part of him wanted to gloat over how he'd figured out who Phoenix was and how to stop Trick and clear everyone's name. The Spirit of Father's Day and the manager, Number One, were missing, but Jack assumed they were on the fifty-second floor, taking care of business with the joker cards.

Looking about the room, the one person he had hoped to see still hadn't emerged. His father was missing, and Jack wondered if his father knew he was there or if something had happened. He caught Sonny's eye as he turned to leave and a voice echoed softly in his head.

*"You're more than welcome to stay and enjoy the festivities of my re-emerging,"* stated the voice in his mind.

Jack turned quickly to see the baby sitting up in his seat, staring at him with a small open-mouthed smile. He walked toward Phoenix, unsure if he should say what he needed aloud or not. He waved at Holly, who smiled at Jack, tilting her head slightly as if approving his part in the solving of the mystery.

"I was wondering exactly what happened to you and the owner of the hotel."

The voice rushed over Jack as if they were thoughts of his own.

*"I remember it all so easily now, but was quite confused as it happened in my older, aged form. I was sitting in my throne, watching the clouds and the sun, able to see the people going about their lives below. My door opened and I wandered out, called by a voice I didn't recognize. Before I knew it, I was on the bottom floor and unable to process where I had come from."* The voice stopped briefly. Jack's hopes rose as he thought Phoenix was about to tell him his father's whereabouts.

*"As for the owner, it seems he is already here."*

Jack turned to look but shortly realized, as he had before, that he, in some way, was the owner. Phoenix seemed to sense his understanding. *"Your father, however, is no longer here. I apologize, but I'm not sure where he is, but he is outside of this hotel."*

Jack tilted his head respectfully, thanking the spirit, and began climbing down the stairs. Sonny followed behind him with her notepad, finishing her notes.

"Why are you leaving?" she asked, stepping down the narrow staircase. The clocks ticked rhythmically with each step they took.

Jack sighed, not answering until they reached the bottom of the staircase. "I don't really feel much for celebrating," Jack said sullenly. "I thought my father would be here, but Phoenix says he isn't at the hotel at all."

After taking the televator back to the fourteenth floor, Jack couldn't help but stare at the wall leading to the April Fool's Day spirit's villa. As he placed his key card into his door slot, he reflected on everything that had happened lately, wondering if he'd missed something. As he entered, he first noticed the room was as he had left it. Everything was in its place and didn't seem disturbed. Since it had been broken into before, he knew he couldn't be too careful.

"So where do you think he is," Sonny asked, leaning against the desk and picking up a folded piece of paper.

Jack removed his flashlight from his pocket and placed it inside the case. He searched his pockets for anything else he may have forgotten, either from a holiday spirit or anyone else. "I'm not sure, anywhere possibly." He removed a button from his pocket, started to place it down, and stopped momentarily. "I suppose it would be easy for Trick to move about so easily without anyone noticing, being able to change his look at will and all." Bringing up the Halloween symbol, Jack remembered what Trick had said to Sonny before they trapped him. He considered how he didn't like discussing his father's death, and he believed Sonny would discuss her mother if and when she wanted.

Sonny wandered over to Jack, who was carefully inspecting the button he had recovered from the roof after the elderly Phoenix had gone missing. "*LR?* Do you recognize it?" she asked.

"I didn't before, but I do now," Jack replied. "It still doesn't make much sense, and it's not exactly the same, but it looks like a televator button. Who would need to make a televator button, and why isn't it a number? I can't understand what it means. Trick could practically teleport anywhere he needed to without it."

Sonny had a puzzled expression as she glanced at the paper she had picked up from the desk and brought it to Jack. "This might have something to do with it."

As he opened the paper, a card fell from it, and Jack recognized immediately what it was. It was the first card he had picked from Luminista his first night at the hotel – a boy sleeping beneath the stars. His hands shook slightly as he remembered what she had said and how much had already come true.

"The fool card. . . . He is the spark that sets everything into motion," she had said. The letter was meant to answer a question he hadn't asked yet. Now, as he read the letter, he wasn't sure what the question was.

"Once for every summer Olympics. Once for every presidential term. Once for every card suit. Once and for all."

Rereading it over and over again with Sonny, he still didn't understand what it meant. He continued to fumble with the button in his hand, thinking of the last question he had asked, believing that had something to do with it.

Writing in her notepad, Sonny asked which floor the button led to. The pad didn't produce a response and, instead, remained blank. "We may need more information as to what the button stands for."

"Once every . . . once every . . . ," Jack repeated. He thought about the last line of the letter, which floors he already knew existed in the hotel, every villa he had come across, and how they corresponded with the year. There was something missing, and it was something so obvious, but it would have to correspond with the letters on the key. Finally it washed over him like remembering the name of an old friend. He smiled before he asked Sonny to ask the pad. "Once every four years — it's a leap year."

"Alright?" Sonny replied, writing down the question in her pad. "It does make perfect sense, except the button has an *LR* imprinted, not an *LY*." When the question disappeared this time, it was able to produce an answer.

"Once every four years following the Gregorian calendar, a day is added to the year. This continues an alignment with the astrological year. The Holiday Hotel follows the weeks and days of the year, and that also includes leap years. This is a secret room only accessible during a leap year. This Leap Room moves from place to place, making it difficult to be tracked. This is the reason the owner has chosen it as his panic room every four years."

"That's where my father must have been," Jack said after reading the pad. He couldn't help but be worried by the idea that, with everything that had happened, his father would choose to hide away in a room instead of helping his son. It wasn't at all how his father behaved. "How can we find a room that moves. . . . And where does this button belong? I haven't found a missing button in the televator yet or one without a number. Not to mention the year is over, meaning the leap year is over," Jack stated, coming to a final conclusion. "It's too late."

A knock echoed on the door. It was the same profound knock they had heard every time they had ordered room service. However, as Jack answered the door, he noticed there was no silver tray with a card. Instead, six attendants surrounded one female attendant carefully holding a small corked vial.

"This is a thank-you gift from the Spirit of New Year's," said the attendant with a number-two badge. "He hopes these five minutes of last year will aid you in your discoveries." The attendant handed the vial to Jack and exited the floor with the others.

As he closed the door behind them, Jack could see a white, grainy material flowing inside the vial. "It looks like the sand from the Infinite Hourglass," he said in disbelief. "Five minutes?"

"Well, that is one problem solved. Perhaps we should try asking Emanuel what he knows about the room," suggested Sonny. After thinking it over, Jack agreed that it was a good idea and accompanied her downstairs. A few attendants along with Father were guarding a caged object. Jack assumed the cage held Trick, trapped in the joker cards. Emanuel was at his podium, finishing a call, when they arrived.

"Be sure to have the Spirit of April Fool's Day released at once," demanded Number One, hanging up the phone and turning his attention to Jack and Sonny. "I am finally able to get business returned to proper order. The authorities are on their way to remove the suspect and place him on trial to be judged by the four city judges. This time they assure us his escape will be impossible and that he will remain contained inside the cards. So, what may I do for our two heroes this evening?"

Sonny approached, waiting eagerly. "We were wondering if you would know how we could get to the Leap Room."

"Or what this button is used in," Jack added.

The manager studied the button and seemed to recognize it, although his response was unexpected. "I was quite curious where it led, myself," Emanuel stated, opening the door behind him. It was the same door he had been locked behind by Trick. The closet was bigger than they had realized. Toward the back they found the reason why it was impossibly large. "Once we were released, I searched the closet for anyone else who may have been trapped. However, I found this instead." Emanuel pushed aside a few items. Behind everything else was a crudely-designed cylindrical tube with a single missing key.

"A televator?" Sonny asked. "You have more than one?"

"No, we do not." The manager smiled slightly. "The Leap Room is made so no one, not even I, has access to it. Someone else has built this televator."

"Who would be able to build something like this?" Sonny asked.

Jack had been quiet most of this time. During their discussion, he'd figured out which pieces of the puzzle were missing.

"Number Two," he said finally.

"Number Two?" the manager asked. "Has she done something?"

"Exactly—she," Jack said in response to their perplexed expressions. "When Sonny and I were disguised as attendants, we ran into Number Two reading a book about panic rooms. I remember it was a guy, and Number Two is clearly a woman. She must've been locked inside the closet too. I also remember Mother's note to the doctor when we got the disguises. It stated the uniforms were just like the other one she had made."

"Someone else was disguised as an attendant besides us and Trick?" Sonny asked. The manager seemed very upset at how many imposters were able to easily fool the guests. "Who do you think it was?"

~ 208 ~

Strolling past Number One, toward the makeshift televator, Jack placed the LR button into the empty hole. "That's what I'm gonna find out," he said, removing the cork from the vial. Beneath the cork, in tiny writing, the message "drink me" was typed onto it. He placed it to his lips, and the sand floated into his mouth. "Whoever it is knows where my father is, so I have to find him."

"A word of warning," began the manager, "Time in the Leap Room is simultaneous, not linear as we perceive it."

Sonny started to say something, but as she did, she began to speak in incoherent words. Jack turned around as she and the manager began walking in reverse toward the door. He was shocked to see himself, as well, staring back at him. Within a few moments, they had closed the door, leaving Jack alone. Besides a few more flashes of light from the door opening again as people climbed out of bags, Jack's focus was on the LR televator button.

Time had been rewound. It shifted backward as images raced by him in reverse. The glow of the button lit the closet in a pale blue. The black outline of an hourglass appeared on his palm, burning him slightly as it counted down the seconds. He had only five minutes to witness what had happened to his father. He entered the televator, pressing the button to the Leap Room. The door closed, and, in no time at all, the machine had powered on, shuddering with strength. The shaking of this televator lasted longer, as if it were searching for the correct place.

Shuddering to a halt, the televator door opened, revealing a new floor that he had never seen before. This one had no doors at all — only an empty, bare hall with a tall generic painting centered across from him. Behind the wall, Jack could hear the scuffling of papers and footsteps.

Removing his flashlight from his pocket, Jack used its light to bend the haze of the massive painting.

It had hinges like a door and blocked the view of a large circular office. The outside windows faced away from the moonlight, and every light had been turned off, making it difficult to see inside the room. A few doors inside led to other areas, but Jack's focus was on the obscured person inside. He didn't know who the person was, but he knew at once that it was the same person who had been posing as Number Two in the staff quarters. In the darkness of the room, his face was well hidden beneath his attendant hat. Jack could barely see anything except the silhouette of a man smashing vases and emptying desk drawers. Papers were thrown through the air, and chairs were shoved over; the desk was overturned. It reminded Jack of the New Year's spirit's villa and his room after they were destroyed.

"Where is it!" yelled the young man furiously. "There're no other places it could be. This is the panic room." His voice sounded young like Jack's, but bitter like the voice of a prisoner who had been locked away for years. He stopped as if he were thinking hard about a particular subject and then continued speaking softly to himself and pacing. "A fake room? If I had my totem, I would be able to see where it is. The remote only allows access once I've . . . found it." He ran to the painting and threw it open.

Jack shuffled back to get out of the way, but the false attendant went through him as if he didn't exist. The false Number Two ran his hand, holding an older, square-styled remote control, up and down the wall across from the painting. As the fake Number Two searched, he continued to speak to himself.

"It must be somewhere here." The remote in his hand began beeping. The young man pressed a combination of buttons and went into the wall. Jack followed using his flashlight.

Inside this wall he could see a door the same size as the painting. It was large, with reinforced bolts and steel bars like a bank vault would have. A button combination lock was placed next to a key card slot. The young man placed his remote control atop the keypad. Removing a key card attached to wires from his jacket's inner pocket, he connected it to his remote control. After he typed a few different button combinations, the remote went into a scanning mode and the door finally clicked. Bolts released, unlocking the door as it swung open, allowing access. As he went in, it shut behind him, resealing itself.

Jack attempted to go through it as well, but his entrance inside was blocked. He attempted to use the skeleton key card, but it refused entrance, repeatedly asking for a code. Words scrolled across the screen, asking him to enter a month and day. Jack could hear arguing inside but just barely. He became eager as he heard a voice for the first time in over a year. His father was speaking.

"What are you doing here?" asked Jack's father. "How did you get in?"

"Where is it?" asked the young man. "Where is the totem? Where is the flashlight?"

Jack was taken aback as he wondered what this strange kid would want with his flashlight. They moved farther away from the door, making it too difficult for him to hear anything. He, instead, focused on the lock code. His fingers trembled at the idea of being so close to seeing his father again as he typed in the first code that came to mind.

Attempting 0229 for the leap day of February twenty-ninth, he was denied with a red light. Next, he tried the day his father had passed away, 1121 for November twenty-first; however, this was also incorrect. Checking his palm, he began to panic, seeing he had just over two minutes left.

He went down a list of possible combinations: his parents' anniversary, the day his father finished his first building, and his mother's birthday. They all came up with the same response. Behind the door, the voices had become violent. Jack was determined to enter the room and see his father. Thinking was difficult as time ticked away. He thought hard about what was important to his father and what the combination could be. The only thing he could think of was when he was always away working. His frustration increased as he thought back to the many times his father had been at work instead of spending time with him. When he finally did come home, his time was almost always spent with Jack, watching old detective shows and movies.

The voices inside had gotten quieter. Jack could still hear scuffling inside. He was running out of time as he stood staring at the cold, unmoving steel. Studying the lock code thoroughly, he could hear the false attendant mention his name. Jack wondered how so much of this seemed to revolve around him and his father. At that moment it became obvious that his father had sent him the flashlight for a reason; and Jack had to find out why. He wanted to know why it was so important; why his father had trusted him with it; and why his father had possessed it in the first place. As he watched his palm tick away the limited amount of time he had left, it occurred to him how he may have been more important to his father than he believed. After he typed in the code 0814, the door clicked, releasing the bolts. As the door swung open,

Jack smiled, realizing how much his father loved him. The code was Jack's birthday.

# Chapter 12
## New Year's Resolution

"What would you possibly want with it?" asked Jack's father. His voice was refreshing to Jack, like the first time he'd seen him after a long business trip. He looked the same as before. He was tall and handsome, wearing thin-framed glasses that hid his pearl-brown eyes and a pinstriped suit with an open-collared blue shirt in Jack's favorite shade. Except for the curly, dirty-blond hair, Jack looked very much like him.

The two men circled a desk inside the room as they spoke. A few monitors against the wall were displaying the floor outside the room, the main lobby, and a few other places Jack didn't recognize. The attendant still hadn't removed his hat, and Jack couldn't tell who it was. Scanning the room, the man continued to hold the remote pointed at his father's chest. With the technology he'd seen already, Jack was sure the remote held a deadly gadget he hoped wouldn't be used.

"That is my business," said the young man, "You should be more worried about your own. This place will be destroyed soon enough if I do not get my totem back."

Jack's father scanned the room, as if searching for something to fight back with. "What makes you think I have it?"

"I have my sources." The young man smiled. "My employer knows it fell into your hands after a long journey. We do not have much time, so either you will give it to me, or I will take it by force."

Jack looked at his palm. There was only half a minute left before midnight. The young man removed a small pouch from one of his pockets. A televator key that had also been in his pocket landed on the ground, but he seemed unaware that it had been stuck to the pouch. Jack's father backed away, to the corner of his desk, and grabbed a small blue orb.

"I was warned someone would come here demanding it," Jack's father said sharply. "That's why I sent it away." He held the orb high, ready to throw it, when the young man used his remote. A green beam of light shot from it and into the orb, and a moment later, it was gone.

"My turn," said the fake attendant, holding up the pouch. As the disguised man threw the pouch, Jack recognized the substance the moment it hit his father. He had been hit hard with a small amount of dream dust. His father stumbled back, spreading items from his desk everywhere as he tried to stay awake. "Since you won't tell me where it is, I'll just have to bring you back to the city with me."

Jack's father found a pen and began scribbling something on a scrap of paper. He hastily wrapped the pen into the note and hurled it out the window, breaking the glass, before passing out onto the floor. The young man opened the bag, which enlarged greatly, and sucked Jack's father into it. Jack ran over, trying to stop him, but he couldn't affect him in any way. The young man tied the bag up as it shrunk back into a small pouch. Pointing the remote toward the ceiling, he teleported out in a flash of green.

Jack checked his palm; only a few seconds remained as Jack sprinted to the window, looking for his father's message. Somehow, it had landed on the ledge after bouncing off the side of the building. Before Jack could reach it, he felt his palm burning hot. Time had run out, and he was losing sight of the room. It felt as if he was being crushed as the room shifted. The floor flickered in and out of sight as Jack noticed Phoenix's destroyed villa beneath him. The televator key the false attendant had dropped fell through the floor and landed on the roof of the hotel as the Leap Room shifted. Jack finally understood that the room was actually hidden above the hotel.

Remembering that the room only existed during a leap year, Jack ran quickly outside the vault door and into the hall. It all began to get fuzzy as he entered the televator. The ground shook hard, as if the world were crumbling away. The lit *LR* key in the televator began to blink, and the moment he pressed it, it went out completely.

He plummeted down. He was forced to grab onto the warped metal walls. Panting hard, he waited for it to stop. The time on his hand ceased to burn, and the time dissolved into his skin. When the shaking stopped, the door opened, allowing Jack back into the closet. Sonny and Emanuel were standing there, and he was almost sure he saw a glimpse of himself before he blinked.

"How did you get over there so quickly?" inquired Sonny.

"I've been gone for a few minutes now," replied Jack. "Thanks, Emanuel. I think I got everything I could." Jack walked out of the closet.

Sonny removed her notepad and pen from her pocket. "Yes, thank you very much, Manny."

"I am not to be addressed in a manner other than my proper name or title, if you please," requested Emanuel.

Smiling as if satisfied with her results, Sonny followed Jack toward the televators. The fountain was now spraying colors of celebration. As they landed, the melody to "Auld Lang Syne" played softly. On the way up to their floor, Jack told Sonny what had happened in the panic room. When he was done, she had only one question. "Where do you think he took him?"

Jack had been asking himself the same question since he left the secret room. "I'm not sure. He could be anywhere," Jack replied, opening his room door.

"Maybe tomorrow we'll be lucky enough to find a good lead," Sonny stated optimistically.

"Tomorrow," Jack repeated. The thought that the next day would finally happen hadn't occurred to him in a while. As he closed his door and climbed into bed, he could feel the effects of the dream dust lull him to sleep. It was quiet as his eyelids became heavy. His mind wasn't racing nearly as much, and before he could have another thought, he was asleep. He got a few hours of peace after so much chaos.

The next morning, Jack awoke with mixed feelings. He was delighted the days would no longer repeat, but he was furious at whoever had taken his father. As he dressed for the day, he wondered how he would be able to be around his father's grave, knowing no one was there. Jack would have no one to listen to his birthday wishes or to look over his mother and him. He couldn't help but wonder if there was something he could've done. Exiting his room, he knocked on Sonny's door, but there was no answer. He was tempted to use his skeleton key card, but thought better of it since she might be getting dressed. Instead, he carried on downstairs in case she had gone to breakfast early.

It was still quite early. Purple, blue, and orange drifted slowly in the fountain. Many of the guests seemed to have either left or were still on the roof celebrating. Either way, there were many attendants on the ground floor who were not in any particular rush, as if waiting for an assignment. The manager, Number One, stood near the entrance with Number Fifty-Two, in a discussion. Jack was making his way over to them when Sonny peered around the west hall with a bag of candy.

"I was wondering when you would be up," she said brightly. "Are you okay to leave?"

Jack nodded slightly. "Yeah, I think so." After checking to make sure his flashlight was in his pocket, they walked over to the manager. His stern expression had softened slightly as they approached the door. The door had reappeared, and through the glass, Jack could see sunlight and the rest area.

"I presume you both are ready to check out?" stated Number-One. "Besides the abnormal excitement, I do hope you both enjoyed your stay."

"Yes, we appreciate everything you have done for us," Sonny said, smiling. She shook the manager's hand as

Number Fifty-Two opened the door slightly. "Thank you as well, Thomas," she added.

Jack's attention was elsewhere as he stared down the east hall. He could clearly see the fortune teller standing by her door, staring at him. As he turned toward her, she smiled. Her door opened by itself and closed shut behind her as she went in.

"Jack, are you coming?" Sonny asked, pointing at the open door. Her hand was outstretched and waiting. Jack thanked Number One and Number Fifty-Two, and after clasping her hand in his, she dragged him through the door the same way they had entered.

Jack awoke in bed, startled at his surroundings. He had the unmistakable feeling of déjà vu, although he had never been through this before. He was in a queen-sized bed with blue-and-white sheets covering him. His luggage had a mess of cards inside and sat beneath a large window overlooking the city. The bed next to him was empty, but he could hear someone in the restroom.

"Oh, honey, you're up," said his mother, coming from the restroom.

"Mom, you're okay?" Jack asked, happy to see she hadn't been harmed. He was confused about how he'd returned to the Blue Mountain Hotel, but at the moment, it didn't seem very important.

"Yes . . . ," she replied. "Why wouldn't I be? Are you still okay to see your father today?" She was dressed in an all-black pantsuit. Jack could tell she had been crying recently, because her eyes were still slightly puffy. She sat on the bed, looking at Jack thoughtfully.

"Yeah, I'm just glad to see you're okay today," Jack responded. He walked over to her and gave her a kiss on the cheek. "Do you mind if I stop by the rest area before we leave, I wanted to check on a picture frame I saw in the gift shop yesterday?"

His mother continued looking at him, holding her cheek as if it had been quite some time since he'd kissed her. "Well, we can stop by there on our way back onto the highway," she said, looking into his eyes. After a moment of hesitation, she spoke again. "It is early. We have an hour or so before the shop opens, so I suppose if you want to go out there for a bit, you can." Jack immediately leaped from the bed. "Just make sure you dress warmly," she finished.

Emerging from the restroom in record time, Jack was dressed and out the door in a few minutes. His hair was still wet, and he heard his mother ask something about him having a new coat, but his mind was on other matters. He began wondering if it had all been a dream—the repeating days, the Holiday Hotel, seeing his father, all of it.

It took almost an hour to walk back to the rest stop as the wind fought back just as strongly as before. Once he arrived at the rest stop, he was able to warm up again. Nothing seemed to have changed as people went about their business. It was still early, but the sun was almost completely out now. Tourists were entering the building because the shops had just opened up.

When he made it to the wall of historical facts about the town, he immediately went over to the photograph of the abandoned building. He still couldn't believe what really lay inside something so old. Instinctively, he brought out his flashlight and began looking at the photo through its lens. With or without the magnifying glass, it all looked the same—until he noticed a faded engraving on the frame.

He could only see it with his magnifying glass handle, but on the bottom right-hand corner, it clearly read, "Built for my son, so we may still have the holidays together."

Jack read it repeatedly, wishing with everything he had that there was a way to get his father back. However, he knew better, and that just made him angry. Being so close and watching him being taken away was almost worse than his father's death.

With the time he had left, he left the rest stop. Outside, the winds hand calmed down in the same familiar way. Walking back up the sidewalk, he stared intently at the abandoned building. The boarded-up black windows and snarling gargoyles had gone unchanged. The foreclosed sign waved slightly, as if gesturing him back inside, but the french doors were secure and shut tight. The gold plaque seemed as if it had aged greatly overnight. The once-pristine gold was now scratched and dirty, as if people had tried to pry it off over the years.

Checking the traffic, Jack ran across the street to get a better look. As he passed the staircase, he heard no sounds of a celebration or rushing attendants. Only the road noise from cars made much sound now. The J.E.T. Enterprises plaque had definitely seen better days as it was now so beat up it could only be legible if you already knew what it said.

Turning to venture back to the hotel, Jack noticed something he hadn't expected to see. Sonny came running up to him with her pen and pad in hand. She still had no coat on — just a regular t-shirt and the ink-stained jeans that she normally wore — as if the cold were an afterthought. Her pink-and-white knit hat still covered most of her hair. Jack could see she was happy to see him as she approached.

"I was hoping you would be here," she said happily. "Did you wake up in your bed, as well?"

"Not exactly, I was back in the hotel bed, not this hotel, but the other," Jack corrected. "How do you think we got there?"

Flipping through the pages of her notepad, Sonny appeared to have some ideas on the subject. "I thought I had perhaps dreamed all of the past ten days. Checking my calendar, I noticed only a day had passed, just as it should have. Now that I see you're here, that theory is out. My only guess is, we returned to where we were supposed to be, as if the repeating days never happened."

"Too bad we didn't ask Emanuel about that before we left," Jack responded.

Sonny surveyed the building, looking past Jack. "No one paid much attention to me when I came here. I thought perhaps we were somehow mixed into the other plane of existence. . . ." She followed Jack's eyes to toward the sky. "What are you looking for?"

"It finally makes sense why we stopped here," he said, more to himself than to Sonny. He continued talking as he stared through his flashlight's handle at the ground up the street. "When we first stopped here, you said you had repeated the same day more times than I had, right?"

Taking a moment to think back, Sonny nodded in agreement. "Yes, a week before you."

Jack continued to scan the ground close to them. "Well, why my mom and I didn't turn off the exit before then, I couldn't understand. I think I do now, though." Jack stepped closer to the road. "Do you see that over on the ground?"

Pointing to the rest-stop side of the street, but farther up the road, he handed his flashlight to Sonny. This made it possible for her to see the trail of dream dust leading to them. It took a few moments, but, soon enough, she could see what Jack had seen. She sprinted across the road of traffic, and, seconds later, she returned with the flashlight and a gold pen wrapped with a note.

"How did you know?" she asked.

"It must have pulled me to come here," Jack replied, examining the object. "My father threw it out of the window as a message, and it popped our tire. But I couldn't see it without the flashlight. Number One said something about time being simultaneous in the Leap Room. That might be the reason I didn't feel the hotel's presence the same day you did, because he wasn't taken until recently."

"So what does it say?" Sonny asked, her pen and pad in hand.

His hands trembling, Jack unraveled his father's note from the pen. J.E.T. Enterprises was etched into the gold. Jack handed it to Sonny. Using the flashlight's handle, he could read the two words written on the otherwise-blank paper. Once he'd read it, Jack handed the paper to Sonny and stared at the unmoving french doors of the abandoned building.

"What does it say?" Sonny asked, unable to see the writing.

Jack took a deep breath, looking at the ground as if he were finding it difficult to control his anger. "Tells me where that guy took my father. I've heard a few of the spirits mention it before."

Hearing the fury in his voice, Sonny glanced up from her notepad. "Where was he taken, Jack?"

"Cloud City," he responded, swallowing a large lump that had formed in his throat as tears swelled in his eyes. As Jack's focus moved away from Sonny, his eyes drifted over to the abandoned building, where the french doors had unlocked, leaving a small slit opening. "Whoever it was or whatever it takes, I don't care. I'm going to Cloud City, and I'm finding my dad."

**Case 1:** *The Holiday Hotel*

**Case 2:** *Cloud City*

## About the Author

Christian N. Wynn was born in Travis Air Force Base, California, and his father's military service took the family all over the United States. For over twenty years he has called Delaware home. The personal experiences of his friends and family are often his most

important inspiration for the characters and stories he creates including the middle grade fiction series, *The Jack Taylor Cases*. This series has been described as *The Hardy Boys Mysteries* meets *The Nightmare Before Christmas*. Along with the *Jack Taylor Cases*, Mr. Wynn's future writing plans include a book series about strange summer vacations, a trilogy of children's books featuring warrior teddy bears, and a book of fables based on characters in the *Jack Taylor Cases* with the profits from the publication being donated to charity.

When he isn't writing, Christian is a movie quoter, binge watcher and enjoys reading written works by Rick Riordan, J.K. Rowling, and Daniel Handler. He's also a Hufflepuff/Ravenclaw hybrid.

You can find more about Christian Wynn and the Jack Taylor Cases at www.jacktaylorcases.com.

www.jacktaylorcases.com
facebook.com/jacktaylorcases
twitter.com/jacktaylorcases

CPSIA information can be obtained
at www.ICGtesting.com
Printed in the USA
BVHW071935280519
549516BV00001B/46/P